"Just tell me, Viking, can you make me feel like that again?" Shay asked.

"Believe it," Dag answered, "again and again and again."

"Ahhh, then I couldn't be splendider."

"Splendider?"

"Oh, yes, and wonderfuller and marvelouser and fantasticker and—"

"Valkyrie, my darling Valkyrie, you'll be all of that and more so. This is just the beginning. Tell me again, a hundred sunrises from now."

"Truly?"

"Oh, yes..."

"Oooohhh...yeeessss..."

Dear Reader:

As the months go by, we continue to receive word from you that SECOND CHANCE AT LOVE romances are providing you with the kind of romantic entertainment you're looking for. In your letters you've voiced enthusiastic support for SECOND CHANCE AT LOVE, you've shared your thoughts on how personally meaningful the books are, and you've suggested ideas and changes for future books. Although we can't always reply to your letters as quickly as we'd like, please be assured that we appreciate your comments. Your thoughts are all-important to us!

We're glad many of you have come to associate SECOND CHANCE AT LOVE books with our butterfly trademark. We think the butterfly is a perfect symbol of the reaffirmation of life and thrilling new love that SECOND CHANCE AT LOVE heroines and heroes find together in each story. We hope you keep asking for the "butterfly books," and that, when you buy one—whether by a favorite author or a talented new writer—you're sure of a good read. You can trust all SECOND CHANCE AT LOVE books to live up to the high standards of romantic fiction you've come to expect.

So happy reading, and keep your letters coming!

With warm wishes,

Ellen Edwards

Ellen Edwards
SECOND CHANCE AT LOVE
The Berkley/Jove Publishing Group
200 Madison Avenue
New York, NY 10016

Second Chance at Love.

LAUGH WITH ME, LOVE WITH ME
LEE DAMON

**A SECOND CHANCE AT LOVE
BOOK**

Second Chance at Love books are published by
The Berkley/Jove Publishing Group
200 Madison Avenue, New York, NY 10016

Author's Note

To those readers who may be visiting Massachusetts' beautiful Pioneer Valley in the future, and who may try to find Beech Village, I must explain now that I made it up. However, you will find many lovely and interesting old towns and villages in that area that are similar in appearance—and in spirit—to the Beech Village I've described herein.

Massachusetts is blessed with what is generally considered to be the best and most highly trained State Police force in the country. Although I've tried to be accurate in describing my "trooper-characters" as dedicated and efficient as such men are in real life, I may have taken a few small literary liberties with procedures. If so, my apologies, everyone! I'd also like to express my appreciation to Trooper Bill Carney of the Concord Barracks for his indulgence and helpfulness when I "seized the moment" and bombarded him with several dozen questions.

chapter 1

SHAY SLOWED THE tow truck and brought it to a stop as commanded by the red and white sign at the end of Fallow Ridge Road. The Sunday afternoon traffic was heavy on Route 202, and, even with her polarized sunglasses, the bright flashes of intense August sun reflecting from the passing windshields made her squint. It was very hot, somewhere in the low nineties, and only the topmost leaves of the trees moved at all in the nearly still air. At ground level there wasn't even a whisper of a breeze.

Hurricane weather, thought Shay, recalling the last weather report she'd heard an hour ago. The third hurricane of the season had started moving out of the Caribbean yesterday and was now on a northward track some seventy-five miles off the Atlantic Coast. It would take only a slight veering to the northwest to bring the big tropical storm slamming into New England. And the one predictable fact about hurricanes was that they were totally unpredictable.

Hunching her shoulders, Shay leaned forward, trying to loosen the wet tee-shirt that was stuck to her back with perspiration. Still no break in the traffic. She stifled a frustrated groan and settled back, idly thinking about the hurricane watch. It had been several years since one had hit New England, and the last two had wreaked their havoc over along the coast. It was rare for one to strike up through this central area of Massachusetts, although older residents still talked about the Big Blow of 1938, which had cut a wide path of incalculable destruction across the state.

"Oh, well," Shay muttered to herself, "with luck it'll stay out to sea. Ah ha, here we go."

There was a break, finally, in the swiftly moving lines of cars, and she swung the tow truck quickly across the southbound lane and turned northward, hitting the switch to activate the truck's orange dome light. Within a few minutes she reached the overlook parking area and slowed down, flipping on her right directional signal. The lot was full of parked cars and wandering people who were trying to find a breath of air. The overlook was at one of the highest points on this stretch of Route 202, and it provided a panoramic view of the Quabbin Reservoir, a man-made body of water—the largest in Massachusetts—that filled a large portion of what had once been the Swift River Valley.

Shay drove slowly along the edge of the parking area, her eyes searching for the late-model green station wagon the State Trooper had described in his call for road service. A van pulled out of the lot just ahead of her, and she saw the station wagon, its hood up, at the very end of the paved area. She parked just behind it and slid out of the truck, automatically tucking the keys into her pocket.

There didn't seem to be anyone near the wagon, and she stood still beside it, head up, searching the area for someone who might be the owner. Her eyes stopped on the tall, very tall, male figure rapidly threading his way through the parked cars, obviously heading in her direction with ground-eating strides.

Oh, no! Much too much! Shay's eyes widened in a rare mixture of alarm and appreciation as she got her first un-impeded look at him, and some protective instinct started flashing a red neon warning in her mind: *Trouble! Shay, my girl, that's six and a half feet of trouble heading straight for you!*

For a few seconds she felt strangely suspended in time as she took in all the details in one sweeping examination: a close-cropped cap of platinum curls, much darker brows and lashes, dark eyes in a lean face that was saved from being too handsome by a slightly crooked nose and a stubborn chin, a pale green tee-shirt and navy shorts that emphasized the well-developed athlete's body and the long, strongly muscled legs. His deep tan made the unusual platinum hair even more startling, and Shay found her eyes drawn back to it momentarily before her attention finally became fixed on his expression.

Reality came crashing back when she saw the assessing, encompassing appraisal he was giving her. She tensed as she watched that familiar predatory gleam light the dark eyes and the firm, slightly sensuous mouth slowly widen in an appreciative smile.

No way, chum. Forget it! Even if you are just the right size, I don't need you or what you've so obviously got in mind. At thirty-two, Shay had seen that expression on too many male faces to mistake its meaning. She sighed resignedly, wondering with only mild curiosity which approach he'd use. Over the years she'd heard them all, and she'd long ago accepted the fact that there was something about a five-foot-eleven-inch redhead, built on Junoesque lines, that brought out the hunter instinct in even the mildest of men.

"Is this your wagon?" she asked, trying to head off the inevitable as he halted two feet in front of her, surveying her with a blatantly sexy smile.

"Hmmm," he murmured. Reaching out with both hands, he removed her sunglasses and breathed, "Oof."

"Oof? Does that mean yes or no?" Shay's voice had a tinge of impatience, since he seemed to be wholly occupied in gazing bemusedly into her eyes. It was unnerving.

"Are they natural, or are you wearing contacts?" he asked, obviously fascinated with the pure aquamarine color of her eyes. "I've never seen quite that clear, light blue-green color before. It's beautiful."

Mildly stunned, Shay opened her mouth and then closed it again. Unwillingly, she laughed and said, "I don't believe it. A new opening line." She tilted her head to one side and looked—up, for a change—at him consideringly. "I've been asked if my hair was natural and if my shape was all mine, but no one has ever suspected me of faking the color of my eyes. It's natural," she assured him as she pulled her gaze away from his. "Now, how about this wagon? Is it yours?"

"Oh, yes, it's mine," he answered, watching her intently, his eyes traveling as if with a will of their own over her slim body and down the long, bare length of her legs. Uncomfortably she realized that her damp tee-shirt and denim cutoffs left little to his imagination.

"What happened?" she asked impatiently. He was making her nervous with that concentrated examination. Or perhaps it was that aura of self-assured masculinity he exuded that was standing every tiny hair on her body on end. "Did it overheat, or have you blown a radiator hose?"

She walked away from him toward the front of the car, leaning over the fender and ducking her head under the edge of the hood to see if the problem was readily visible. Intense heat was rising from the front end, and she knew better than to try to touch anything bare-handed.

She sensed him behind her, but when he remained silent, she looked over her shoulder and asked again, "What happened? Look, I really don't have all afternoon to mess around here. I'll try—"

"Super Mom?" he interrupted, staring fixedly at the back of her tee-shirt.

Shay backed a step from the car and straightened up, turning to face him. "My youngest son gave it to me. He's a bit prejudiced. Listen, Mr. . . . Do you want me to do something about your car or not?"

At the mention of a son, his eyes had dropped to her ringless left hand. Now, ignoring her question, he scowled at her and growled, "You're not married, are you?"

It was tempting, and it would be the easy way out. She toyed with the idea for a few seconds, but something told her he'd check it out, so she finally muttered resentfully, "I'm a widow, not that it's any concern of yours. Can we—"

"That's a relief," he sighed, smiling approvingly at her.

"Oh, good grief!" Shay exploded as she saw that he was taking another visual tour of each of her seventy-one inches. "Will you please, please, pay attention! Do you or don't you want to get your car going?"

"Don't worry about it," he said absently. "Someone will be along soon to take care of it. I'm more interested right now in getting to know you better. Where would you like to have dinner this evening? There's a rather nice place I know of in Amherst. Quiet, soft music, great food. They do a very nice filet mignon. What time shall I pick you up?"

Shay blinked at him with a strong feeling of disorientation. She wondered for a moment if she were getting sunstroke. It was very hot, and she'd long ago passed the stage of perspiration; she was now definitely sweating. Somehow, they seemed to be carrying on two separate conversations, and she infinitely preferred sticking to hers.

"May I have my sunglasses, please?" she asked, gesturing toward his left hand. "Thank you. Now, if I may also have your undivided attention for a moment? Yes. Well, I'm the someone who is here to get your car going. That," she waved toward the tow truck, "as you can see, is a tow truck. It also contains various tools for effecting emergency or temporary repairs." She paused to see if he had any comment to make. Her rising temper was not appeased at the sight of a charmingly indulgent smile on his face, exactly the sort of smile one would bestow upon an exceptionally clever child. She gritted her teeth and snarled. "Look Mr. . . . whoever you are, it's been a long day, and I'm hot, sweaty, and tired. I've left my sons in charge of the station, and I'm in no mood to stand around here in this blistering sun so that some rude Don Juan can look me over like—"

It happened so fast Shay barely had time to blink. One instant he was smiling delightedly, and before she could get the next word out, he was reaching for her with a heated, purposeful gleam in his dark sherry eyes. Before her mind had time to change gears, her quick reflexes brought her hands up to brace, none too gently, against his rib cage. It stopped him before he could get close enough to do more than wrap his extremely large hands around her waist.

For a few long moments they stood unmoving. Shay's scrambling mind tried to sort out the jumble of strange bits of input it was receiving and get itself back on track. She stared at him wide-eyed and saw his predatory look change first to rueful surprise and then to amusement. She felt off-balance, overheated, and totally nonplussed at her momentary impulse to slide her hands around that warm, strong chest and take the long step into his arms.

My God! I don't even know his name! I don't want to know his name. I want to get as far away from him as . . . no way . . . it's been years since I've reacted like that to a man and even then . . . frustration, that's all it is . . . maybe Mother's right about my leading an unnatural life . . . on the other hand, I sure don't need a macho man like this one setting me off. Must watch that. Well, face it, Shay old girl, you have been watching it. But, then, who would have expected a complete stranger to come on like some conquering Viking? Her lips twitched involuntarily at the appropriateness of "Viking," and she flicked a quick look at the cap of silvery curls.

Her eyes were caught by his amused gaze, and she scowled at him, reversed her recent decision, and demanded, "Who are you, anyway?"

"Dag Haldan," he said mildly, smiling warmly into her stormy eyes. "And you?"

"Shay MacAllister," she mumbled reluctantly. She would have liked nothing better than to refuse to tell him, but it would have been useless, since "MacAllister's" was emblazoned in foot-high red letters along the side of the tow truck.

"Shay." He seemed to savor it for a moment and then said, "I like it. It suits you. Do you always wear your hair like that, wrapped around your head in those braids? It's such a beautiful color, it would look much better loose. How long is it?"

"I don't believe any of this." Shay stared at him with a slightly bewildered expression, then shook her head and searched the ground around her feet. "Where are my sunglasses? I think I'm getting sunstroke. I came out here to fix a car and—"

"Here." He reached behind her and picked up her glasses from the fender. She didn't even bother wondering how they got there. "Wait," he said as she started to turn away. "What about tonight?"

"What about your car?" she countered, mentally throwing up her hands and deciding that two could play at cross-conversations.

"First things first. What time shall I pick you up?"

"What are you going to pick me up with?" she asked sweetly.

"All right, we'll talk about the car," he conceded, adding with an unrepentant grin, "first."

Knowing it was a mistake to encourage him in any way, she still couldn't help smiling back at him. Over the following half-hour, while she did a temporary repair job on the radiator hose and filled the radiator, she found herself relaxing even further under his obvious interest in what she was doing and how she had learned to do it.

In answer to his questions she told him about her grandfather who had built the small garage and gas station in the 1920s, both because he was fascinated with cars and how they worked and because he figured that no matter how bad things got people would always need to buy gas and get their cars repaired.

"Is he the one who taught you to fix cars?" Dag asked.

"Mostly. He was my father's father, and he taught Dad all about cars when Dad was growing up. However, Beech Village is quite small and a bit off the beaten track, and the business couldn't support a second family. So, when my folks got married, Dad went to work for a trucking firm in Springfield. I was almost six when Dad got out of the service and we moved back here. Grandma had died, and Gramps had developed arthritis in his hands, so he couldn't manage all the repair work by himself. Dad took over most of the work in the garage, and we all moved into Gramps's big house."

She straightened up and closed the hood. "There. That should hold long enough for you to follow me to the garage. It's only about ten miles. I think I've got a hose the correct size, and it'll just take me a few minutes to install it."

Apparently in no hurry to leave, Dag leaned against the car, watching her wipe her hands with a clean rag. "Finish telling me about your grandfather."

"You can't possibly be all that interested," said Shay repressively. A delayed reaction seemed to be overwhelming her—or perhaps it was the heat and her long busy day. Whatever the cause, she suddenly felt cross as crabs with both herself and this too tall, too handsome, too appallingly sexy man. She still couldn't believe that she'd almost allowed this total stranger to kiss her. Yes, kiss her. Of course that's what he'd intended to do, and for just a moment there she'd actually wanted to feel those sinewy arms holding her and that wide, warm mouth on hers. *You've been in the sun too long, gal.*

"Could we be on our way, now, Mr. Haldan? I don't like to leave the boys on their own for too long," she said coolly as she started toward the truck. "Just follow me. If your temperature warning light comes on, give me a toot and pull over."

Shay glanced back in time to see his eyes, narrowed speculatively, following the slight swing of her firm hips as she walked away from him. She spent the next twenty minutes lecturing herself on why she did not want to get involved with a man, any man, but particularly that man. By the time Dag parked outside the garage, Shay was waiting for him, flanked by her tall redheaded sons, and again exuding her usual self-assuredness and air of independence.

Unfolding himself from the confines of the wagon, Dag smiled at the boys as he straightened to his full height.

"There's certainly no mistaking whose sons you are," he said, looking from the boys' interested faces to Shay's wary expression. He lifted an inquiring eyebrow at her and drawled challengingly, "Aren't you going to introduce us?"

Her eyes flashed as she bit back an instinctive "No!" After all the time she'd spent instilling manners in the boys, it wouldn't do at all for her to be rude to someone who was, in their eyes, a stranger. After all, they had no way of knowing just how provoking this pushy Viking had been, and she wasn't about to tell them. *Drat the man!*

With her hands on the boys' shoulders, she said, "This is Marcus Severin, my oldest," nodding to the boy on her left who was almost as tall as she, "and this is Kyle," she added, smiling down at the very freckled redhead who just reached her shoulder. "This is Mr. Haldan. It was his car that was broken down."

"Hi. Pleased to meet you," said Marcus, stepping forward to offer his hand. He was very thin, but obviously healthy and bubbling over with energy.

Shay saw the interested once-over Dag gave the boy

before he asked, "I don't suppose you play basketball, do you, Marcus?"

"Yeah, I do. It's my favorite sport," Marcus said slowly, looking at Dag intently, a dawning recognition in his eyes.

Before he could say anything else, Kyle grinned and held out his hand, exclaiming, "He's a super player, Mr. Haldan. He's going to be on the freshman team this fall."

"I'm going to try out for it, Kyle," corrected his brother, still staring at Dag, his eyes now fixed on that cap of platinum hair.

"Oh, Marcus, you know—"

"I know who you are!" Marcus cried excitedly. "You're the Norseman!"

"He is?" squeaked Kyle. "Are you?" he asked Dag, his eyes nearly popping in wonder.

Laughing, the big man nodded his head, admitting, "I used to be."

"Oh, wow!" breathed Marcus. "Wait 'til I tell the guys I met the Norseman. Right here at our garage."

"What's the Norseman? Or who?" Shay asked in some bewilderment, looking from her very excited sons to her oversized blond nemesis.

"Aw, Mom, where have you been?" Kyle wailed. "He's a basketball player. He's great! Wicked fast and he never misses!"

"Well, that's not exactly true," Dag protested, "but thanks for the compliment."

"Gee, Mom, don't you ever listen to us?" Marcus asked plaintively. "I know I've talked about him. He plays for the pros, or he did." He turned back toward Dag. "Did you really retire? Aren't you going to play anymore at all? You still look in great shape."

"Hmm, do I?" Dag's eyes locked with Shay's, and his mouth widened in a slow smile as he saw the flush of red in her cheeks.

With some effort, she pulled herself together and her eyes away from that laughing brown trap. "Listen, why don't you guys go have a cold drink of something and talk basketball while I get Mr. Haldan's car fixed. I'm sure he's anxious to get on his way."

"Oh, I'm in no hurry," Dag said blandly. "It's always a

pleasure to visit with fans, especially young ones. Now that I've retired, I don't get as much opportunity to talk basketball as I used to. And I'd love a cold drink."

"Super. Come on over to the house," Marcus invited. "It's just across the Green."

"Nana made lemonade, and there's still a great big pitcher left," chimed in Kyle, bouncing with excitement. "And we've got a basketball hoop out back. Maybe you could show us some neat shots." He tipped his head way back to gaze hopefully up at the very tall man.

"Sure. Sounds like fun," Dag said, smiling at the young boy and dropping a large hand companionably on his shoulder.

Shortening his long stride to accommodate theirs, Dag followed the boys' lead across the station yard toward the road. After a few steps, he glanced back over his shoulder at the watching Shay, gave her a knowing grin and a wink, and called, "Be back in a while. Then we can finish our discussion."

"Why does that sound like a threat?" Shay muttered to herself as she stared after her adored sons, who were enthusiastically and unknowingly thwarting all her plans for quickly getting rid of that far-too-friendly Casanova. From the snatches of conversation drifting back to her on the still air, it was evident that he was cleverly drawing the boys out about their family history and life-style.

"Damn!" she groaned, stalking into the garage to find a radiator hose. "Ten to one Mother will turn to mush, too, and by the time he gets through charming the eyeteeth out of everyone, he's going to know a lot more than I want him to."

Shay drove the station wagon partway into the garage so that she could work in the shade. Although it got her out of the direct rays of the blistering sunlight, it did little to cool the overheated state of her mind. She stewed, fumed, swore under her breath, and finally flung a flat wrench at the wall.

It's not always true that redheads are temperamental; but Shay knew that in her case, her bright, flaming, uncompromisingly red hair was an early warning signal for a short-fused, blazing temper. When she was very young, her male classmates had quickly discovered how easy it was to taunt the leggy tomboy—who could out-run, out-jump, and out-climb them all—into an awesome rage. Shay's parents were rather less than awed when the complaints started filtering in from outraged mothers. Although her father seemed secretly amused at some of her methods of retaliation, he recognized the need for teaching his feisty daughter either to control her temper or let it out in ways that didn't result in decorating the young male population with black eyes, chipped shinbones, and temporary bald spots. Thus, by the time she was eight—and with the aid of some fatherly incentive applied to the seat of her jeans—Shay had developed a number of ways—some of them downright diabolical—of both coping with her temper and keeping her youthful adversaries in line.

Now, many years later, she stood in the middle of her garage and thought longingly of how satisfying it would be to grab a couple of fistfuls of those platinum curls and . . . *I wonder if they're as soft as they look. Oh, come on, Shay! And what do you think he'll be doing while you're snatching him bald? Just remember the size of those hands. If he should decide to grab fistfuls of you—Well . . . under other circumstances that might be interesting. No. Forget it. You're managing just fine, old girl, without any entanglements. And that man definitely has tangling on his mind.*

"You, Mr. Norseman, are just going to have to find another court to play in," she murmured resolutely as she banged the hood down on the wagon. "There, now, all set and ready to go. And the sooner the better."

Glancing at the clock as she headed for the sink to scrub her hands, she realized that her workday was almost over and wondered when her blond nemesis intended to come back for his car. If he thought for one minute that she was going to drive it over to the house for him and give him a chance to delay his departure, he'd just better start thinking again. Maybe she should call and have her mother tell him it was ready. Or perhaps—The shrill ring of the phone interrupted her plotting.

"Oh, no, not another road call," she muttered, striding into the office and snatching up the phone. "MacAllister's!"

"No need to snap my head off, dear," chided her mother.

"Sorry, Mother, I . . . ah . . ."

"Never mind. I told that lovely young man I'd call and have you bring his car over when you close up. Why haven't you told me about him, dear?"

"How could I, Mother? I just met him this afternoon," Shay responded patiently. "And, please, don't get all excited about him. He's going to be on his way very shortly, and I doubt if we'll be seeing him again." She tried to inject a rock-firm note into her voice, knowing from four years' experience that her mother would soar with optimism at the smallest hint that Shay might be interested in a man. Phyllis MacAllister was a firm believer in marriage as the only "proper" and "desirable" existence for a woman, and she deplored Shay's determination to raise her sons and manage on her own.

"Now, Shay, do be sensible. With just a little effort on your part, I'm sure you can catch his interest. He's so lovely and tall, dear—just think, you could wear heels when you go out. And the boys seem to be delighted with him. They've all been out playing basketball. Did you know he was a professional basketball player? He just retired a few months ago. They make quite a lot of money, don't they, dear? And he looks about the right age for you."

"Mother! Good Lord, I haven't had more than a few minutes of conversation with the man, and you've got us practically engaged. Will you stop it! I'll probably never see him again, and I'm not all that sure I want to anyway."

"Well, of course you do. A handsome man like that, probably comfortably fixed, and he gets along so well with the boys. Don't be silly, dear. Besides, everything's all arranged. Now you just hurry along over—don't forget Dag's car—and get changed into a nice dress and—"

"Wait! Wait a minute, Mother. What's all arranged? Mother," Shay demanded, suddenly filled with foreboding, "what have you done?"

"I haven't done anything, dear," said Phyllis blandly. "Dag made the arrangements. I just knew you'd be pleased. He's so anxious to take you out to dinner this evening—I really think you've caught his fancy, Shay—and I knew how much you'd enjoy getting away from everything for an evening, so of course I assured him you'd be delighted."

"But, Mother, I don't—"

"Oh, don't worry, dear. I've taken care of everything. I've pressed that lovely sea-green dress, just to freshen it up, and laid out all your things. All you have to do is shower and dress. Shouldn't take you any time at all. You'll have plenty of time to get there by seven—that's when Dag made the reservations for."

"But—"

"We'll talk later, dear. If you hurry along now, you'll even have time to shampoo your hair and do something more elegant than those braids. Oh, Shay, he's such a nice man!" lilted Phyllis, and Shay felt that familiar sinking sensation at the note of excitement in her mother's voice. *Oh, Lord, here we go again!*

"Yes, isn't he?" Shay said rather flatly. "I'll be along in a few minutes. 'Bye, Mother, and . . . ah . . . thanks for doing my dress."

Shay hung up the phone gently, then picked up a pencil and methodically broke it into small pieces while wrathfully condemning that "nice man" to a terminal case of poison ivy.

I knew it. I just knew he'd get around her. Dripping charm and sweet-talk and flashing that damn smile. And he's probably got the boys all whipped up with enthusiasm. So, how do I get out of this?

"You don't, you twit," she muttered, violently punching the No Sale key to open the cash register. "You know what'll happen if you go over there and say you're not going. Mother will look bewildered and tearful, and the boys will think you've lost your mind. They're probably itching to tell all their friends that their mother is dating the Norseman, and he's teaching them the fine points of hook shots or whatever. Sneaky beast! He *knew* I didn't want to go out with him!"

chapter 2

"...THE MOST UNPRINCIPLED, underhanded, unscrupulous—"

"Oh, please, not unscrupulous. I was perfectly honest with your mother and the boys, and they were all sympathy and helpfulness when they realized how much I wanted to take you out to dinner, and how hesitant you were to desert them on such short notice." Dag's voice was slightly choked as he tried valiantly to hold back his laughter. He diverted his attention from the road for a moment to cast an amused look at the fuming woman beside him. As his eyes met Shay's stormy gaze, he no longer restrained his satisfied smile.

"Don't give me that smug grin." Shay growled. "You knew very well that I didn't want to go out with you. I just *knew* it was a mistake to let you loose with Mother and the boys. What did you say to her? She thinks—"

"She thinks I'm interested in her stubborn, bad-tempered, contradictory, independent but altogether fascinating daughter, and she couldn't be more relieved." He managed, with obvious effort, to keep his expression as bland as his voice.

"Bad-tempered!" snapped Shay in a tone only two decibels below a yell. "I'll have you know that I have a perfectly delightful disposition . . . except with overbearing, arrogant,

domineering men who think they know what I want to do
better than I do and—"

"I'll bet you kiss nice, too," Dag commented, carefully
keeping his attention fixed on the winding road.

"I . . . what?" gasped Shay. She stared at him in dismay
while her mind scrambled frantically for a fast change of
subject to head him off this particular track. Her "Where-
arewegoingtoeat?" came out in a breathless tumble of words,
rapidly followed by a squealed "What are you doing?" as
he pulled over to the side of the road and flipped the gearshift
into Park.

"Satisfying my curiosity," he murmured as he turned
toward her.

Shay had no more than time for a startled "What—"
before she found herself hauled across the seat and into his
arms. One large, warm hand closed around the nape of her
neck, holding her head still as his mouth came down on her
parted lips. At the first touch of his tongue on hers, her
already confused thoughts went skittering off in all directions, and her mind filled with slow, swirling sensations.

*Heat . . . his breath fanning across her cheek, his mouth
and tongue teasing hers, tempting her, taunting
her . . . strength . . . his arms and hands, holding her, moving on her, pressing her breasts into the muscled hardness
of his chest . . . softness . . . the silvery curls tickled her palm,
clung to her searching fingers . . . need . . . the hot, honeyed
uncoiling deep in her vitals sending its messages, urging
her arms around his shoulders, arching her back to bring
her closer to the warm, sinewy length of him . . .*

The raucous blast of a two-note claxon from a passing
car brought them abruptly back to a belated sense of time
and place. Shay blinked open passion-clouded eyes and
stared dazedly into the hot, sherry-brown eyes only inches
away.

It was his look of pleased satisfaction that snapped Shay
out of her heatedly dreamy state. In rapid succession, her
emotions cartwheeled through chagrin, shock, self-disgust,
and, ultimately, fury. *Not again! What is it about this damned
Viking that absolutely destroys every bit of my self-control
and resistance? He puts his hands on me and . . . POOF!*

"Damn you, you're a witch!" she yelled, pushing him

violently away and scooting back to the far side of the seat.

"Warlock," Dag corrected, grinning smugly.

"See? You even admit it," she snarled, jabbing an accusing finger at him.

"No, no, sweetheart. I'm only correcting you. A male witch is a warlock, and whyever would you think I am one?" He cocked a curious eyebrow at her.

"You must be. There's no other explanation." Shay threw her hands up in a gesture of disgust. "I never, never have any trouble keeping men at arm's length, but you...you are some kind of throwback, Dag Haldan. You just charge right in like a damn Viking raider and chop down all opposition. You might just as well wear one of those horned helmets and carry a battle-axe!"

His roar of laughter did nothing to cool her temper, but he seemed to make a supreme effort to control his mirth when he saw her clenching her long, strong hands into very businesslike fists.

"Don't...don't take a swing...at me, honey," he gasped. "You'll break...at least a finger or two. Ohhh, you are something else, Shay MacAllister. A Viking raider! As if I'd attack you!" Still grinning, he reached for her hands, closing his own much larger ones around her fists and refusing to let go despite her strong tugs. "Easy now, honey. Quiet down and tell me something."

"What?" she asked warily. She was only half aware of his strong, supple fingers working hers out of their clenched position while his thumbs stroked soothingly over her palms. The rest of her mind was frantically replaying her last outburst as she realized, with dawning dismay, just how much she'd given away to him.

"The truth, now. No fibbing." He seemed to be fighting to keep a serious expression on his face. "You don't really dislike my kissing you, do you?"

Shay stared at him in consternation. *Oh, no! He knew! Oh, you dimwit, of course he knew. How could he help it? You were melting into puddles all over him. Well, you don't have to admit it. Sure, Shay. Tell him you hate it, and watch him fall over in hysterics. And if he should by any chance believe it, maybe you can try to convince him you're a fragile five-foot-two. Idiot!*

Game to the end, she decided to try evasion. "Ahh, listen, Dag, we're starting to run late. Didn't you say our reservations were for seven? It's twenty of, and—"

"Do you or don't you?" he asked insistently, pinning her with his intent gaze.

"Can't we discuss this over dinner?" she asked plaintively. "I'm really getting hungry. It's been a long, busy day."

"We'll be on our way as soon as you answer the question," he said reasonably.

Shay's lower lip started to jut stubbornly until she caught the interested gleam in his eye. With a mental shrug she gave up and said grudgingly, "All right, so I don't dislike it. But that doesn't mean I want you to keep on doing it!"

"Why not?" It was an interested inquiry, casually tossed at her as he released her hands, put the car in gear, and angled back onto the road.

"Why not?" she echoed. "What kind of a question is that? I just don't want you to."

"Come on, sweetheart, you can't just leave it there. You've got to have a reason. You know as well as I do that we practically send up smoke signals. You can't just ignore an attraction as strong as this without a reason." He threw her a quick, encompassing glance, no doubt taking in the signs of her tension and distress. "You're too far away," he complained in a deep purr. "Come over here next to me."

"I'm fine where I am. Just concentrate on driving, Dag. It's almost seven."

"Stop worrying about the reservations. They'll hold them. I can concentrate much better if you're closer," he coaxed.

"Dag—" Her protest broke off as he slowed the car and steered toward the side of the road. "What are you doing now?"

"Stopping," he said reasonably, "so that I can devote both hands and my full attention to persuading you to indulge my—"

"Oh, never mind the syrup," Shay growled. "I'll move over. But only for the sake of getting to my dinner before I expire from hunger," she warned, sliding over to the middle of the wide seat.

Dag glanced down at the three inches of space still between them, but when he lifted his gaze to her face and encountered that jutting lower lip, he seemed to settle, for the moment, for her compromise. Shay switched on the radio and made a great play of being totally absorbed in a phone-in talk show.

She wasn't even hearing the heated discussion over the new gun law. Her mind was assimilating, debating, and assessing the increasingly disturbing ramifications of her reactions to the stranger slouched comfortably behind the wheel. Granted, she had been a long time without a man— and not just in the physical sense. It had been a long, dry spell since she'd had any emotional involvement, either. Even before Cary had died in a motorcycle racing accident four years previously, their emotional ties had been severed. In the last two years before he died she'd seen him only twice, and both meetings had been brief.

She caught herself staring at the large hands resting on the steering wheel, remembering with vivid recall the feeling of them spread across her back. Strong hands. Safe hands. Oh, sure, she told herself, until the crunch comes and he wants to be off and away to play in a more interesting sandbox. So maybe he's not a Cary who'd rather live in a truck and race motorcycles than raise his sons. And he doesn't look like the type to clean out the savings account and take off into the wild blue, leaving his wife broke with the rent due and two kids to feed. But there'd be something. A new woman? Younger, prettier, cuddlier, sexier? Shay was stunned at the strength of feeling—a mixture of loathing, reproach, and possessiveness—that tore through her at the thought of Dag putting those hands on another woman.

My God! This is ridiculous! For all I know he could be married. Or engaged. Or living with someone. I don't know beans about him, really. Six hours ago I didn't know he existed! Overkill, that's what it is, you twit. You've never had a man come on so strong. You've never even met a man like this one before. Definitely out of your league, Shay MacAllister. And you can't blame your absolutely shameless response to him on plain old sexual frustration. You've been frustrated for years, and none of the other men who tried their hand raised even a mild interest. Well, maybe a smidgen once or twice, but not enough to tempt you into doing any-

thing about it. Not even enough to inspire anything remotely like that abandoned kissing you were doing with him. Maybe he really is a warlock. There's got to be some reason for the way he dissolves all your defenses in ten seconds flat.

"Shay! Are you all right?"

"What?" she asked bewilderedly, coming abruptly out of her preoccupation at the sharp sound of his voice. She turned to look at him questioningly, wondering why he'd practically yelled at her.

"I asked if you were okay. You had the strangest expression on your face, as if you were in pain."

"Oh. No, I wasn't . . . I'm fine. I was just thinking." She wrenched her eyes away from his mesmerizing gaze and looked around, finally realizing that the car was stopped. The sprawling Victorian-style inn, set in the midst of green lawns and riotously colored flower beds, looked coolly inviting. Now that the car was stationary and the breeze generated by its movement had ceased, Shay could feel her skin dampening in the heavy, hot air. The heat of the day, unusually intense for late August, had only slightly abated with the coming of evening.

"Bother! You didn't tell me we were eating *here,*" she complained, looking ruefully down at her simple polished-cotton sundress. With its narrow shoulder-straps, low square neckline, and beltless waist, it was certainly cool, but it was not the kind of dressy costume usually on display in the inn's elegant dining room.

As Shay slid out of the car and stood beside him, Dag let his appreciative gaze drift from the bright red hair, restrained in a smooth French pleat, down over her full breasts, supple waist, curving hips, and long legs, until his eyes finally rested on her slender feet encased in high-heeled white sandals.

"Amazing," he murmured appreciatively. "You have the loveliest feet. I've never been much on feet before, but I could learn to love yours."

"Good heavens," Shay muttered, torn between embarrassment and delight.

He looked up and seemed rather jolted to find himself almost at eye-level with her. It was, no doubt, a unique experience for him, Shay reflected. In heels, she was only four inches shorter than he.

"Mmmm. Dancing with you is going to be a most interesting experience." The gleam in his eyes told Shay more clearly than any words that dancing was not the only experience he was anticipating. His smile was totally outrageous as he gave her another quick once-over and said softly, "Don't worry about your dress. With your height and the way you move, you'd make a gunnysack look elegant."

Determined as she was not to give in to his charm, Shay still couldn't hold back a gurgle of laughter. With a slight shake of her head she resigned herself to the futility of fighting against Fate—at least for the moment—and let him take her hand and lead her up the brick walk.

By the time she was comfortably seated in a rattan armchair, facing Dag across a matching glass-topped rattan table, her initial dismay had disappeared and had been replaced with intense curiosity. Although they had not arrived until seven-forty-five and both the indoor and outdoor dining rooms had been full, the hostess had immediately shown them to a corner table on the screened veranda. She had not only addressed Dag familiarly by name, but had given him what sounded almost like a report on the evening's business in the dining rooms. He had remained standing and talking quietly with the hostess for a few moments after Shay took her seat.

Slowly sipping a glass of white wine, Shay relaxed in her chair and watched Dag as he scanned the dining rooms, his gaze pausing every so often on an employee or a particular table. She had stopped worrying about her dress. She didn't know whether it was due to the unseasonably muggy evening or the fact that it was still the tourist season, but the majority of the diners were casually dressy rather than elegantly so.

Shay suddenly realized that she had been staring at Dag for several minutes, and she made an effort to pull her eyes away and fix her attention elsewhere. Not that he wasn't worth staring at. He had extracted clean clothes from his luggage in the back of the wagon. At the urgings of Marcus and Kyle, he'd used their bathroom to shower and shave and had eventually reappeared in tailor-made gray slacks, hunter-green silk jacket, and pale green silk-knit shirt. Shay also suspected that his black calfskin shoes were handmade. She well knew the problems of finding ready-made clothes that properly fit extraordinarily tall figures. With a mental grimace she chided herself for the untypical flash of envy at Dag's ability to afford custom-made clothes.

"Why are you scowling at me, now?" Dag's voice held just a faint trace of exasperation.

"It wasn't really meant for you," she said, smiling apologetically. "Just something I was thinking about." Before he could question her further, she turned to look out over the grounds. "This is such a lovely place. It must take a lot of work and money to keep the gardens and shrubbery so beautiful. Is that a swimming pool down there past the rose garden?"

"Yes," Dag answered absently, his mind obviously on another train of thought. He set his wine glass back on the table and leaned toward her, reaching out to take her hand. "Tell me about your marriage, Shay."

"What?" She stared at him in shock. It was not the sort of question one asked a stranger, and it was the last thing she'd expected him to say.

"It wasn't exactly the made-in-heaven kind, was it?" he asked quietly. "Now, don't blame the boys—they didn't mean to give away family secrets—but while we were shooting baskets, they made a couple of comments that led me to believe they'd never spent much time with their father. At least, he didn't seem to have taken them to any kind of sports events, or to have played with them, or even talked much with them."

"Dag—" Shay stopped and bit her lip, turning her head away from that penetrating gaze to look out over the gardens. After a few minutes she started speaking softly, almost to herself, her eyes still fixed on the flowers now barely discernible in the deepening twilight.

"I had just turned eighteen when I graduated from high school, and I'd been accepted at UMass for the fall semester. I was all enthusiastic about studying engineering, and, oddly for a girl my age back then, I wasn't terribly interested in young men. Probably because I'd spent most of my life positively towering over most of the available males. In any event, I was green as grass and in no way prepared to cope with the craziness of Southern California."

"How in the world did you end up there?" Dag interjected.

"Mother has a sister who lives just outside Los Angeles, and she invited me out to spend the summer with her. It was sort of a reward for doing so well in school and being valedictorian at my graduation, and I guess partly a last fling before starting the hard work of college. So I packed up and went off with my aunt's assurances ringing in my ears that there were lots of tall boys in California and that I'd have a great time."

"Did you?"

"Oh, yes. Aunt Evie introduced me to a whole clutch of young people, mostly the sons and daughters of her friends, and I leaped right into the swim of things. And, yes, there were lots of tall boys as well as an incredible number of tall girls. For the first time in my life, I didn't feel like a freak. It was terrific."

"And then?" Dag prompted as she paused, searching for words.

Why am I telling him this? I don't even know him. Because he asked you, dummy, and he's obviously interested. Why should he be? Oh, Shay, don't be such a dunderhead.

"Shay?"

"Er . . . yes . . . well, I met Cary Severin the second week I was there. Fourth of July weekend. A group of us went down to Baja camping, and he was with another crowd that camped near us. We hit it off right away and spent most of the weekend exploring around by ourselves. He lived only a few miles away from Aunt Evie's, and we started going out together four or five times a week, spending most of the weekends touring around Southern California. He was a few years older, in his last year at UCLA, and . . . well, somehow, at the end of the summer, we decided we were in love and couldn't stand to be at opposite sides of the country, so we went up to Nevada one weekend and got married."

Dag raised a sardonic eyebrow and murmured, "Given

the life-style of the young at that time and place, I'd say you made a rare decision . . . ah . . . or did you have to make it legal?"

Shay scowled at him and growled, "No, we didn't *have* to get married. I just made it plain that I wasn't going to stay out there with him unless we did." She waved a dismissing hand as he opened his mouth to comment. "Don't say it. So I wasn't totally in the swing of the west coast free-for-all. Just as well, since I ended up getting pregnant within a couple of months. I guess that was the beginning of the end. Cary, with typical male arrogance, assumed that I knew how to take care of such possibilities—which, of course, I didn't. He was mad as hell—kids weren't in his planning—and he took off for several weeks to stay with a friend. Luckily, I was earning enough to pay the rent and feed myself until he decided to come back. It kind of went along like that for a few years. He'd be around for a while, and then he'd take off for a while. I never knew when he was coming or going. He—"

"Didn't he work? How did you manage with two kids?" Dag interrupted.

"He had a degree in Phys. Ed., and he worked off and on as a coach for various sports. He probably did other things, too. I don't know. He never told me much about what he was doing, except for the motorcycle racing. He got hooked on that after we'd been married a couple of years, and he started going off on the racing circuit and spending most of our money on bikes and gear."

"When did you break up? Your mother said that you'd had a terrible time even before he was killed—that he'd left you flat."

Shay shook her head in exasperation, realizing that her mother had done just what she'd feared and had melted under his blasted charm, spilling all sorts of things. "I guess you could say that. We'd been married, if you could call it that, about eight years when he finally decided that he'd had it. He cleaned out all the joint bank accounts and took off with all his possessions—and a few of mine. At the time, I'd been out of work for a couple of months because Kyle had had appendicitis and I needed to stay home with him until he recovered. There were some complications, and it took a while before he could go back to school. It was one big mess. Thank God, my landlord was a sweetheart, and he waited for the rent until I could find a job."

"What did you do?"

"Same thing I'd been doing—worked as a mechanic!" Shay laughed at his stunned expression. "Well, it was the best-paying job that I was qualified to handle. I didn't know beans about typing and office stuff. Thanks to Dad and Gramps, I was a good mechanic, and it never took me long to find a garage owner who was willing to hire a woman. That was one good thing about Southern California; it's such a crazy place, it's easy for a woman to do things she might have trouble doing in more conservative areas. Anyhow, I was able to earn enough to start saving some again, and when Cary was killed two years later, I had enough to get us back here."

"From what your mother said, you came back just in time."

"Yeah, we did. She'd been using a manager to run the station since Dad died, and it wasn't working out too well. He wanted a bigger cut than she could afford to give him and still keep up the house. I sent him packing and took over the business myself. We're not making a fortune, but with all of us sharing the house, it's plenty to pay the bills and bank a bit for the boys' college expenses."

Empathy, thought Shay as she met his warm brown gaze, and why do I feel as if the elevator just dropped ten floors? She could *feel* the waves of understanding and compassion rippling toward her. With an automatic tensing, she could also sense the questions crowding the tip of his tongue. She sent up a silent plea that he'd keep them there.

Watching Dag debate with himself over whether to push her to fill in the yawning blanks in her mini-biography or to wait until she was lulled with food and wine, Shay became aware, for the first time in over half an hour, of her exceedingly empty state. Her hollow condition was brought to Dag's attention when her long-suffering stomach growled protestingly.

"Good heavens," he exclaimed. "Why didn't you say something?"

"I did," Shay pointed out. "I distinctly remember—"

"Never mind. Here's something to take the edge off," he announced as a young waiter arrived at their table and placed a lobster cocktail in front of Shay before serving Dag with a plate of cherrystone clams.

Shay's eyebrows rose in surprise as she stared at the array of succulent lobster chunks. "When did I order this?" she asked Dag is some bewilderment.

His flashing white smile would have warmed the heart of any dentist, and it had much of the same effect on Shay's long-restrained libido. "I put our order in when we arrived," he answered blandly. "Your mother told me that you loved lobster cocktail."

"Too true. What else did my mother just happen to tell you?" Shay muttered in despair. *Mother, you blabbermouth, we are going to have a very long talk first thing tomorrow. Lord, what else did you give away?*

"If you're trying to find out what's coming next, it's filet mignon with sautéed mushrooms, fresh asparagus, and baked potato skins."

"Oh, yum! Baked potato skins? With crumbled bacon and sharp cheese?" she bubbled gleefully.

It seemed to take Dag a moment to find his voice, and then it was slightly hoarse. "I can't remember ever seeing anyone get so excited over something like potato skins. It usually takes at least sapphires, if not diamonds, to stir up that much enthusiasm in the women I know."

"Now what would I want with diamonds?" asked the ever-practical Shay. "I'd look damn silly pumping gas with diamonds dripping all over me."

"Oh, I don't know," Dag drawled. "In some circles it's the 'in' thing right now to dress up designer jeans by wearing a fine gold chain-bracelet with a single diamond dangling from it. Very chic, very restrained. Nothing less than a carat, you understand. Stop laughing, Shay. Would I make that up? Woman, you really are out of the swim of things out here in the country."

"It has nothing to do with living in the country," Shay protested, still laughing. "It's just that I find some of the current styles ridiculous. I haven't yet come to terms with the idea of spike heels with jeans, never mind adding sporty diamonds as the ultimate in casual wear."

"You're not going to try to convince me that you don't like diamonds, are you?" Dag asked with a cynical twist to his mouth. "There isn't a woman born who doesn't get sticky-fingered at the sight of jewels."

"Nonsense!" Shay stated heatedly. "A great many women don't particularly care for diamonds, and I'm one of them. I think diamonds are cold and blah. No color, no warmth—they just sit there and glitter."

"You sure that's not just sour grapes?"

Giving him a look that should have charred his silver curls, Shay bit back a crude retort and relieved her feelings by viciously stabbing her fork into a chunk of lobster.

Cool it, girl. It just won't do to fling the silverware around in here. Wonder what the hell is biting him, though. He didn't seem the sarcastic type up to now. Hmmm. Maybe it's the women he's been hanging out with. A pro athlete, well-known, good-looking . . . okay, okay, handsome . . . probably pots of money and invitations to all the fancy places . . . face it, he's had more than his share of butterflies. They always flutter around the big-name athletes in swarms. He's probably used to women hinting for jewelry and expecting him to take them first-class. If you're smart, Shay, you'll make sure this is the last time you go anywhere with him. Forget all that bone-melting sex appeal. You don't need him, in the first place, and in the second place, he's way out of your league. Just keep saying it.

"That lobster's already dead, Shay. There's no need to attack it." His amused voice and deep chuckle brought her attention back to the moment, and she looked up to find that his mood had switched again to affectionate indulgence with just the tiniest hint of male challenge.

"One can never be too careful with shellfish," she replied blandly. "Tell me, Dag, why did you decide to become a pro athlete?"

With an I-know-what-you're-doing-and-I'll-go-along-for-a-while look, he began discussing his basketball career and, within a few minutes, had her laughing at his stories of some of the more outrageous pranks dreamed up by his teammates to stave off the boredom of road trips. Shay aided and abetted him for all she was worth in keeping the conversation on his experiences for the remainder of their dinner. It wasn't until they were served coffee and Cointreau that he tried to bring up personal topics again.

chapter 3

TOYING WITH HIS liqueur glass, Dag asked with seeming casualness, "Did something happen in your marriage to turn you off men? You're a very attractive and appealing woman, and yet your mother says you rarely go out."

Shay met the warm concern in his eyes with a feeling of dismay. It was obvious from the intent look on his face that he was not asking simply out of idle curiosity. Much to her surprise, she found herself loath to fob him off with "None of your business," which was her first instinctive reaction. On the other hand, she barely knew him and yet had already told him more than she'd ever intended to reveal about her marriage. She had the uneasy feeling that he'd done a lot of reading between the lines.

Stalling for time, Shay slowly sipped her coffee and then tossed the ball back into his court by countering with her own questions.

"What about you, Dag? You've been asking me all sorts of personal questions, but you've said very little about your own life." Shay lifted her left hand and began ticking items off on her fingers. "How old are you? Are you married, separated, divorced, or single? Why did you retire? What are you going to do for a living? How—"

"Whoa!" Dag commanded, laughing and grabbing her hand. Wrapping his fingers around hers, he rested their linked hands on the table, resisting her halfhearted efforts to pull away.

"Oh no, sweetheart. You have to give me time to answer the first batch before you go through your fingers again. Now, in order, I'm thirty-six, never been married, retired because I'm moving out of my prime for pro sports, and haven't quite decided what I'm going to do next."

Shay propped her chin on her free hand and fixed him with a look of frustrated amusement. She was almost thankful for the jumble of questions his less-than-satisfactory answers had raised, since it gave her something to concentrate on besides the distracting movements of his fingers over her hand.

"Would you care to fill in some of those gaps?" she asked chidingly. "For instance, how come you never married? What do you mean—"

"All right, all right, Madame Curious!" Dag exclaimed, laughing. "Well, let's see, why did I never marry? I came close a couple of times in my first few years in the pros. It's something like inhabiting another world when you get into professional athletics—especially if you catch the fancy of the public and the press. Before you're halfway ready for it, you're a superstar, and suddenly you've got people all over you—mainly women. And not just the groupies, but..." Dag flipped a hand in the air as he frowned in concentration, apparently groping for the right words.

He leaned toward Shay, fixing her with suddenly serious eyes. "It's something of a shock to find yourself being sought after, almost hunted, by celebrities and beautiful women. It was all too easy to take it seriously and... but I was one of the lucky ones, thanks to my very practical parents and their very down-to-earth midwestern upbringing. Before I went too far overboard, I realized that all those people weren't really interested in me as a person, but in me as a superstar and a very public, very highly paid media pet. All those eager, charming women were far more interested in being seen with me and in receiving expensive little gifts than in developing any kind of serious relationship."

Shay watched him closely but could see no signs of conceit. Rather, his manner was one of rueful self-awareness, and the direct gaze he had fixed on her clearly indicated that this was a man who held to his own values and didn't need to prove anything to anybody.

Suddenly Shay remembered his odd reaction to her comment about not liking diamonds. Her brows drew together as she demanded, "Is that what you think of all women? That we want expensive gifts? Did you think I was putting you on or playing some kind of game when I said I didn't particularly like diamonds? What kind of woman—"

"Easy, now, don't get all wrought up," Dag soothed, reaching across the table to place two quieting fingers against her lips. "No, I don't think anything of the sort about you. Although, if you consider how many gold-diggers and rich-husband-hunters I've met, you have to admit I have reason to be wary."

So have I! Shay watched him suspiciously as his eyes drifted over her, the appreciative gleam in their sherry depths matched by the smile widening his tempting mouth. *Tempting? Shay MacAllister, it is high time you got out of here and back to your own world.*

"I . . . uh . . . it's . . . ah . . . getting late," she stammered, wondering where her normally cool control had gone. She waved a nervous hand at the darkness outside and began edging her chair back from the table.

With a series of smooth moves that left her blinking, Dag had her on her feet and strolling with him across the dining room, his deep voice murmuring in her ear, "It's far too early to go home, sweetheart. We'll have a drink in the lounge and listen to the music for a while. There's quite a good group playing, and if you stop scowling at me I just might dance with you."

They were at the entrance to the lobby, and Shay stopped short, spinning around, ready to tell him exactly where and how he could dance. Her irate words died in her throat when she found him turned away from her, deep in conversation with the hostess. He had, however, taken the precaution of clasping her wrist in an unbreakable hold.

Fuming, Shay restlessly shifted her feet and tugged uselessly against his restraining grip. After a few minutes of futile effort, she acknowledged that, unless she was willing to blow up a scene in front of half-a-hundred people, she was not going to get away from him. She steadfastly refused to recognize the insidious voice in a forbidden corner of her mind that chanted: "You like it. You don't want to get away. You're hooked, hooked, hooked. Too late, Shay, too late."

"No," she whispered to herself, "it's impossible."

She turned to look at him and met the smiling mockery in his eyes.

"It's not in the least impossible," Dag murmured, freeing her wrist and sliding his long arm around her waist, urging her toward the entrance to the lounge. "Another drink won't hurt you at all, since I'm driving, and just think how much you'll enjoy dancing with someone taller than you."

The lounge was dimly lit, and Shay only caught part of the motion as Dag attracted the cocktail waitress's attention and indicated an empty table. He then guided Shay in the opposite direction, toward the small dance floor.

With her concentration fixed on avoiding chairs and people, Shay didn't have a chance to protest until they reached the edge of the floor. And then it was too late. Turning quickly to tell Dag that she would much rather just have a drink and then leave, she found herself wrapped in his arms and swung easily into the middle of the slowly moving dancers before she got out more than "I don't—"

For the first time in her life, Shay was at a loss as to how to handle a man. She didn't want to dance with him, be in physical contact with him, or even to spend any more time with him. From the moment she'd seen him striding across that parking lot, she'd been totally aware of him, not only as a handsome, virile man, but also as a powerful, determined, and predatory male force that called out to something deeply female and sensual within herself. She'd never before reacted to a man in this way. Always she was in control of herself and the tepid relationships she'd allowed with the few men she dated.

This man was not going to allow her to control anything, Shay moaned to herself. And somehow, when he touched her, she wasn't all that sure she wanted to. Not even in the earliest days of their marriage, before disillusion set in, had Cary been able to make her feel so aware of the basic nature and needs of male and female. *Chemistry, that's all it is. It can't be anything else. Not so fast. Can it?*

The music was seductive—a slow, dreamy medley of Rodgers and Hammerstein love songs—and, despite her better judgment, Shay found herself relaxing under the subtle strokings of the large hands on her back and the feathery touch of Dag's warm lips against her ear. She wrapped her arms loosely around his shoulders, telling herself, unconvincingly, that there was no place else to put them. She ruthlessly silenced the tiny voice that insisted on pointing out the lovely feeling of her breasts pressing against the firm muscles of his chest, and how marvelous it was to be able to dance cheek-to-cheek without bending her head.

It was no use. The insidious spell of the soft, smoochy music, the dim lights, and, most of all, the warm, lithe body moving sensuously against her were rapidly weakening her resistance. It dissolved altogether as she felt his hand press insistently down over her hips to the base of her spine, allowing her no escape from the insinuating movement of his firm thighs against hers. With an unconscious sigh of surrender and an instinctive shifting of her hips to fit more closely to his, Shay lost herself again in his arms. *This is becoming a habit!* was her last coherent thought for several minutes.

"Shay, my little love," Dag finally whispered in a near gasp, "you're going to have to cooperate with me in this. Another thirty seconds and we'll be providing one hell of a floor show."

"Hmmm?"

"Shay! Loosen your arms, darling, and help me put some space between us."

Blinking her eyes open and scowling protestingly, Shay slid her hands across his shoulders and rested them against his chest, feeling the slowing beat of his heart. She gradually became aware of his hands enclosing her waist and holding her a few inches away from him. Still moving slowly to the music, they stared at each other with an identical questioning look in their eyes.

Shay struggled to gather her skittering thoughts together and get them under her usual practical control. Not for a moment did she believe that her interpretation of the look on Dag's face was anything but wishful thinking. Lust, yes. There was no question but that they had a powerful sexual attraction for each other. But that was all. It had to be all. There was no room in her life for another disaster like Cary. She'd finally managed to get her world sorted out and organized, and there was no way she was going to get involved with another man. Not now, not ever. Especially not with this man. Besides, involvement wasn't what he was after. She hadn't missed his casual, comfortable manner in the dining room, the way he seemed to fit into these expensive surroundings as if he'd been born to them. Custom-made clothes and probably custom-made women. This wasn't her world, and she didn't even want to try to enter it. No matter how tender and loving he might look, she knew it was nothing more than a well-practiced seduction technique, and she was not—*was not*—going to be fooled into thinking there was anything more to any of this than a desire to get her into the nearest bed.

"I won't," she growled, glaring at a startled Dag.

"Now what are you in a temper about?" he asked. "I haven't made an indecent proposition all evening. As a matter of fact," he added thoughtfully, "I don't believe I've made one at all. So far, the only invitation I've extended was to dinner. However, since you've brought it up..." He tilted his head and smiled invitingly.

"Me? I haven't brought up anything!" she gasped, outraged. "You've made it perfectly plain that you... I mean, you didn't have to say anything... that is, every time you look at me, you... you get that damn gleam in your eye, and what about kissing me? You can't say that wasn't an invitation!"

"Mmmm. You know, I think you're right. It was; and such an interesting answer you gave me, too." He laughed at the wrathful expression on her face and suddenly pulled her back into his arms, wrapping them around her in a hard, quick hug before he swung her away from him, grabbing her hand and leading her toward their table.

"Behave yourself now, sweetheart," he said softly. "Just look at that couple seated near our table. Why don't we set them an encouraging example of true togetherness? Hmmm?"

Shay looked into the handsome, laughing face so close to her own, and her stomach suddenly felt much like it had the last time she was on a roller coaster. There was a sensation of inevitability about it, a feeling that she was caught up in something she wasn't going to be able to brush off as a fleeting aberration. Oh, it was all a total confusion, and she'd think it out later. Right now . . . right now, what would it hurt to enjoy some of that togetherness? Just for a little while.

Back at their table, Dag made himself comfortable on the Victorian loveseat next to Shay. She was all too aware of the long length of warm male thigh resting against hers, and the possessive arm curved around her shoulders. It was not conducive to carrying on a coherent conversation. Neither were the husky-voiced endearments and loving comments that were directed at her every few minutes, accompanied by a truly remarkable range of seductive, amused, wry, and teasing looks. Helplessly, Shay responded to the sensual web Dag was weaving around her, and she suppressed her clamoring warning signals with the mental assurance that it was only for a little while.

His idea of togetherness seemed to involve being in contact with as much of her as was possible. By the time they were ready to leave the inn, Shay found herself, much to her shock and dismay, actually missing him for the few moments it took him to close her car door and walk around to slide into his seat. Perhaps that accounted for her dazed acquiescence to his coaxing, "You're too far away. Come over here."

They were turning from the inn's long access road onto the highway before she was aware of the soft brush of hair against her bare arm, and she looked down to discover that at some point Dag had removed his jacket. In the dim glow of the dash lights, she could see the ripple of muscles in his arm as he shifted through the gears. The car was a closed world, and when she raised her eyes to his strong profile and saw the corner of his mouth twitch in a small smile, she knew he was spinning his spells again. Somehow, just then, it didn't seem to matter, and she didn't protest when he drew her hand over to rest flat on his leg and covered it with his own much larger hand.

"You have such strong hands, Shay. It's a surprise every time I notice how graceful they are. I like them." He slanted a glinting look at her, and she knew he was remembering how she'd dug her fingers into his shoulders and back when he kissed her.

"Thank you." It was time to change the subject.

"That dining room hostess," she said thoughtfully, "sounded like she was giving you a report. How come?"

"She was . . . sort of." Dag gave her a quick, assessing look before continuing, "I own a piece of the inn. In fact, I'm living there at the moment."

"You own The Colonial Muster?" Shay's voice rose to a squeal.

"Only partly. I'm in partnership with an old friend of mine. He does all the actual managing; I'm mostly a silent partner."

"But—I don't understand this. You're not originally from around here, are you? Even I would have heard of a local celebrity like a pro athlete."

Dag chuckled at her aggrieved tone. "No, love, I'm not from around here. I grew up in the midwest, but I've lived mostly on the west coast, since both the teams I played for were out there. However, Dan Crawford, my college roommate and still my best friend, is a New Englander, and I've always spent some off-season time here with him. Then, four years ago, my sister and her husband bought a motel-marina complex on Lake Winnipesaukee in New Hampshire, so I've been spending even more time in the east."

Shay was almost afraid to ask the question, and one part of her—the sensible part—hoped the answer would be negative. "Are you . . . are you going to be here much longer?" She had her eyes fixed on the big, tanned hand covering hers.

"As a matter of fact, I plan on staying here permanently. In this area, that is; not at the inn. I've been looking around this summer, in between other things, for a house. This is a good, central location for me, and I like the countryside."

Trying to cope with her mixed feelings of dismay and elation, Shay's next question was a bit breathless. "What . . . what do you mean 'central'? Central for what?"

"I . . . ah . . ." Dag waffled for a moment, then seemed to decide to be open with her. "You see, sweetheart, it's like this. I've made a lot of money over the last ten years or so, and I've been investing most of it with the help of Dan's expert advice. He has degrees in business management and economics, and he spent several years as an investment advisor. When The Colonial Muster came up for sale a few years ago, it was on a downhill slide, but Dan knew the owners and the problems and was sure he could turn it around. We went into partnership to buy it, and he left his New York job to come back here to manage it. Since then, we've bought two more old inns—one in the Berkshires and one just outside Bennington, Vermont—and restored them and put them back on a paying basis. I also provided some of the backing money for my sister and brother-in-law when they bought their place at the lake, so I get a cut of that and occasionally give them a hand if they need it. That's where I was coming from today."

"But if you're mainly putting up the money for these things and other people are managing them, what do you do with yourself? I can't believe you just cruise around killing time and picking up strange women."

Dag's deep laugh brought goosebumps out along the length of Shay's spine, and she couldn't restrain an answering grin.

"It does have a certain appeal, but since few of them would be in your class, I'm sure I'd get bored within a week or so," said Dag, still chuckling. "Right now, I'm keeping reasonably busy with a series of basketball camps that I've been running with a couple of other pro players. I'm not sure yet just what I'll be doing this fall and winter. Find a place to live, for one thing, and Dan and I are looking into a few possibilities. I want to keep some free time for skiing." He hesitated before adding, "I guess I'm in an enviable position right now: I don't need to work at any one thing to earn a living, so I can take my time to pick and choose some interesting things to get involved with. If they make money, fine. If they don't, that's okay, too, as long as it's something worthwhile. Maybe something involving kids; I've always liked working with kids, and there are some interesting programs for teaching handicapped children how to play variations of most popular sports."

Shay gave him a considering look, remembering his easy

way with Marcus and Kyle. "I bet you'd be terrific at that sort of thing. Are you thinking of something like the Special Olympics?"

"Along that idea, maybe. I'm still looking into the possibilities. Right now, though, I'm more interested in getting some answers from you."

Startled, Shay suddenly realized that they had stopped, and she looked around in some bewilderment. Expecting to see her own yard, she was momentarily disoriented as her vision encompassed nothing but shadowy space and a sweep of starlit sky. Then her searching gaze discerned the glint of water far below, and the shadowed masses became defined as wooded hills. They were, inexplicably, parked on the overlook above Quabbin Reservoir where they had met ten hours ago.

"What are we doing here?" Shay asked suspiciously.

Lifting her hand from his leg, he brought it to his mouth, turning it so that he could trace a delicate pattern on her palm with his tongue. He easily countered her instinctive move to jerk her hand away from him and smiled lazily at the signs of incipient temper in her flashing eyes and gasping breath. Before she had time to get out the first explosive word, he flipped open his door with his free hand and started to slide out of the car, pulling her after him.

"Let's walk."

"Walk?" Shay gasped as she scrambled to catch her balance. Tugging her skirt straight with her free hand, she scowled at her captor, who still maintained a firm hold on her other wrist. "Do you realize it's after midnight? I have to be up at six in the morning."

His only answer was a fond smile as he led her inexorably to the walkway bordering the overlook. Shay balked, grabbing at the top of the protective wall edging the walk and using it an an anchor.

"Dag! Will you please be reasonable?" With great willpower, she restrained the impulse to give him a swift, attention-getting kick in the shin. In the patient tone she used with the boys when they were being contrary, she said, "I appreciate your wanting to show me the lovely view, and it is a bit cooler up here. However, it is also getting late,

and I've had a long, busy day and...the evening out...
dancing and all...well, it's been very pleasant, but I really
must be getting home now."

Shay watched him expectantly, feeling quite proud of
her air of cool restraint—especially since every sexual sen-
sor in her body was twitching and tingling in reaction to his
proximity. One long step and she'd be in his arms. She
willed her feet to take root. If she'd learned one thing this
evening, it was that this devastating man could turn her
carefully organized life upside-down. Temporarily. He'd
made it plain that he wanted her physically, but she doubted
that her unsophisticated attractions would hold his interest
for long.

*And why should that thought hurt, you ninny? You've
held out for years against offers for quickie affairs. Remember, girl? No more involvements with men? Give 'em
an inch and they'll interfere in your whole life. Except when
you need them, and then where are they? Long gone and
to hell with responsibility. You can only depend on yourself.
Keep saying it. It took you long enough to learn it—the
hard way.*

"Dag? Please? I really would like to go home now." Her
voice was low and slightly pleading as she tried to interpret
the almost somber look on his face.

"You're right," Dag said contritely. "I'm sorry. I'd forgotten what a strenuous day you put in, and now I've worn
you out with a long evening."

Shay looked at him uncertainly, not quite sure of the
tender note in his deep voice, but she didn't pull away when
he let go of her wrist to put his arm loosely around her
shoulders and lead her back to the car.

They rode in companionable silence to Beech Village.
Shay's long day was catching up with her, and she was half
asleep.

The village was dark and quiet with only a few lights
showing the houses around the Green. The night was very
warm and still; not even a breath of air stirred the dark
masses of the trees. Letting the big wagon coast along Shay's
drive, Dag brought it to a stop beside the side porch and
turned off the engine. They got out quietly and walked on

the grass beside the walk to the steps. Shay tried not to let her heels click as they crossed the porch and stopped by the door.

When she turned to say good-night, she found Dag just inches away from her, and she caught her breath as the familiar excitement raced through her. Her "Thank you for the evening" was a whispered stammer, and then everything went dark as Dag reached past her shoulder and switched off the porch light beside the door.

Her "Oh" was a soft expulsion of breath as his arms closed around her and his warm mouth and seeking tongue unerringly found her half-parted lips. Lulled by the security of being on her own porch, she didn't even try to fight her instincts. Her hands pressed against his back, her fingers kneading the taut muscles, while her arms wrapped tightly around him. Lost in the hot interplay of their mouths and tongues, she was only vaguely aware of his hands sliding down to curve around her bottom and pull her into the thrusting urgency of his hips. The blaze of answering heat deep in her vitals had her squirming against him and moaning helplessly into his mouth, while the last vestige of coherent thought disappeared in a red, sensual mist.

She came back to dreamy awareness at the sound of his voice whispering in her ear, and she found that she was leaning against the wall, held there by the pressure of Dag's hips and one long muscular thigh thrust between hers. Somehow, her dress had been pulled down, baring her breasts to the exploration of his large, warm hands, while she had evidently pulled his shirt loose so she could stroke the smooth, damp skin of his back.

"Shay...sweetheart...this is no place to make love ...please...come back to the inn with me...oh, God, you're beautiful...your breasts feel so good...just like I knew they would...please, love...come with me..."

Whether the ringing in her ears was from her blood rushing through her veins or from her belated internal warning bells, Shay neither knew nor cared. It was enough that it started bringing her out of the sensual web enmeshing her. As Dag's hoarsely whispered words began to separate and make sense, she struggled to bring her mind and body back under control. For long moments, she hovered on the brink, see-sawing between her body's clamoring needs and her mind's insistent "No!"

Even as she brought her hands around to exert steady pressure against Dag's hipbones, trying to ease him away from her, her back arched, lifting her breasts to the seductive stroking of his fingers. Both of them were breathing hard, and their skin was flushed and damp with arousal. Shay knew she didn't have the strength to push him away, and in desperation she finally managed to find her voice.

"No . . . Dag, shhh . . . please, stop now . . ." she pleaded huskily. "Please, we have to stop this . . . I'm sorry, I'm sorry . . . I didn't mean to . . . Dag? . . . Please?"

With a muffled groan he shifted his weight away from her, moving his hands up to grip her bare shoulders and resting his forehead against hers. His breath rasped out in warm gusts across her face as he fought for control. With one hand Shay pulled her dress up to cover her breasts; she lifted her other hand to push back the heavy hair tumbling around her face.

"Oh, damn," she groaned. "You've pulled my hair down. It'll take forever to get the tangles out."

"Let me see it," Dag coaxed, his breathing finally easing. He straightened up and with a few swift motions had her dress back in place and rezipped. It was so dark at the back of the deep veranda that she could barely make out the silver glint of his hair. The sudden glow of the light as he switched it on blinded her. She felt him swing her around, and then his hands were lifting and swirling the thick waves of her waist-length hair.

"God, it's beautiful!" he murmured wonderingly. "Why do you keep trying to hide it?"

Blinking at him as her eyes adjusted, Shay could just make out his delighted smile and the appreciative gleam in his dark eyes. Her face lit with an answering smile as she drawled, "You've got to be joking! How could I hide hair that color? I just try to keep it under control; otherwise, it flies all over the place and ends up in knots."

"Mmmmm." Dag gathered it all up in his hands, then let it go and watched the fiery mass cascade down. "You'll wear it down when we make love, won't you, sweetheart?" he cajoled. "If I promise to help you brush out the tangles afterward?"

"I . . . you . . . oh!" Shay stared at him speechlessly, unable to suppress a flashing series of erotic vignettes.

Dag's grin was smugly aware as he watched the tide of pink spreading across her face.

"But not tonight," he stated, turning her resolutely toward the door and pushing it open. "I want much more time than this to make love with you properly. And I certainly don't want to have to leap out of bed at dawn. Such a waste! Didn't you know that sex and sunrises are one of the most enjoyable combinations yet discovered?"

"Dag! I'm not going to . . . I can't . . . it's just impossible!" Shay had the distinct feeling that she was back on that roller coaster again.

"Not really, love, but it will take a bit of planning. Don't fret about it—I'll work something out." Holding her hands firmly in his, he leaned forward to press a quick, hard kiss on her half-open mouth. "Go get some sleep, honey. You're going to need lots of energy. I'll see you tomorrow."

chapter 4

SHAY'S MONDAY STARTED with bad news and went rapidly downhill from there. She was so tired by the time Dag left, that she fell into a deep, sound sleep within seconds after her head hit the pillow. Not even the doubts, confusion, and questions roiling around in her mind could keep her awake. She was too tired to cope with any of it and decided it could all wait until she was in better shape to deal with the shambles that impossible man was making out of her life and libido. Tomorrow. She'd definitely do something about him tomorrow. It was her last thought.

Not surprisingly, she overslept in the morning, and it took five rings of the phone at six-fifteen to bring her far enough out of sleep to fumble over her night table for the receiver.

"'Lo," she mumbled.

"Shay? This is Tony Clinton. You awake?"

"Uhnn," she groaned, pushing herself up on one elbow. "Wait a minute." Blinking and yawning, trying to snap her groggy mind to alertness, she sat up and swung her bare legs off the bed, bracing her feet on the floor as she stretched.

"Okay, Tony, I'm awake. What's up?" She reached for the pen and pad of paper beside the phone, expecting this to be a wrecker call. State Police Sergeant Anthony Clinton was often the shift commander on the midnight-to-eight shift at the nearby Barracks.

"If you open your eyes and look out your window, you'll see what's up," came the sardonic answer. "The wind, my girl, is definitely up . . . to twenty miles an hour with gusts of thirty-five to forty. I'm just calling now to alert you."

"Has that hurricane swung our way?" she asked. She had the phone tucked between her cheek and shoulder as she struggled into her robe. Now that she was fully awake, she realized how chilly it was in her room. Last night it had still been hot and stuffy, and she hadn't bothered wearing anything to bed. The sharp smack of rain against the wide windows brought her head around, and she expelled a disgusted "Damn!" as she saw the tree tops whipping against a low, leaden sky.

"We just got an advisory from the Weather Bureau," Tony said. "The storm veered west shortly after midnight and hit the Carolina coast a glancing blow north of Hatteras, then swung back out to sea and started moving northeast again. Right now we're getting the fringes, but there's a strong chance it might swing back to the coast somewhere in New England."

"How big is it, Tony?"

"Some eighty miles across, winds around the eye have gone up to a hundred and twenty, forward speed's around thirty-five miles an hour. It's a beast. If it comes inland we're going to be in one big mess."

"Aren't we just," Shay muttered, still staring out the window. "Okay, Tony, what do you want me to do?"

"Batten down your place and the garage this morning so you'll be ready to move out if it hits. I know it's a little early to go to all that trouble, but the Weather Bureau warned us that this storm is very erratic. If it does hit us, we'll need you and the wrecker on the highways, and you won't be any help to us if you get trapped in the village by downed trees."

"You want me to leave here before it hits?" she asked in surprise.

"Right. We're still in the middle of tourist season, among other potential problems, and some of these people either aren't going to hear the warnings or won't pay any attention to them. You can imagine what'll happen to any cars that are on the roads in the middle of a hurricane. Believe me, we're going to need you."

"All right, Tony. I'll get everything nailed down here. Do I keep checking in or what?"

"We'll have a man ready to contact the emergency personnel. He'll call you as soon as we're notified that it's coming our way. If you have to go out on a call, keep your radio on. Wish you'd get a CB."

"Don't need one. Thanks for calling, Tony. You'll understand if I say I hope I don't have to see you later."

"Why, Shay, you know you're always welcome to drop in any time." He was laughing as he hung up.

Shay was wide awake now, and her practical mind was starting to sort out priorities and organize the battening-down operation. She walked across to the large bay that curved out in a three-quarter circle at the corner of her room, from which she had a panoramic view through the three sets of tall, double windows.

The MacAllister home was a twenty-room Victorian, built in 1883 to replace the original 1768 homestead, which had been destroyed by fire. With the advantages of skilled local carpenters and a plentiful supply of seasoned hardwoods from his own mill, Angus MacAllister didn't have to stint on either the size or number of rooms, porches, bays, turrets, stairs, closets, and random nooks and crannies. As a result, the sprawling, three-storied house was an explorer's dream for children and an unending nightmare to clean.

When Shay's parents received an unexpectedly large profit from the sale of some of their land for highway construction, they replaced the doddering heating system, re-piped and re-wired the house and barn, remodeled the kitchen and three existing bathrooms, and added a first-floor powder room and a master bath.

As she stood in the bay scanning the front and side yards and what she could see of the Green and the village through the wind-whipped trees, Shay rapidly reviewed the present state of the house, barn, and grounds. With a scolding hiss at herself for dawdling, she ran for the bathroom. Twenty minutes later she skipped down the back stairs, following the welcoming smell of pancakes and sausages to the kitchen.

"'Morning, everyone," she said with forced cheerfulness, crossing the big room and dropping into her seat at the old round oak table. "What kind soul closed my windows before I drowned?"

"Hi, Mom," Marcus and Kyle mumbled past mouthfuls of pancakes.

"I did, dear," said Phyllis MacAllister, half turning from the stove. "The wind coming up woke me around five. You know how it whistles around those eaves at the far corner. I just got my windows down when the rain started, and the boys woke up when I went in to close theirs. You were so sound asleep, I doubt if anything less than the roof coming down would have disturbed you."

"Ummm." Shay finished her cranberry juice and pushed the glass to one side. "The phone finally did. Didn't any of you hear it?" She looked questioningly at the boys.

Marcus swallowed hastily before answering. "We were all outside rescuing Nana's pot plants and the hanging plants on the piazzas."

"And we forgot the folding chairs last night, and they blew all over the yard," chimed in Kyle.

"Is this the hurricane, Mom?" asked Marcus, his dark eyes wide with excitement.

"Oh, dear, we're not going to get hit are we?" Phyllis exclaimed in alarm.

"We might, Mother. Right now, we're just feeling some long-range effects. That's what my call was about." Between bites of pancakes with blueberry syrup, Shay told her interested audience about Tony Clinton's call. By the time she was sipping her second cup of coffee, Marcus and Kyle were bright-eyed and bouncing with excitement, while Phyllis was nervously tapping the table and looking more worried by the second.

Although she was ostensibly listening to the boys, Shay was very much aware of her mother's restlessness and wondered at the cause. She knew that Phyllis had been through hurricanes before, and she found it hard to believe that the possibility of another one would unnerve her.

Ever since she and the boys had moved from California to live with her mother, Shay had developed a much deeper understanding of Phyllis as an individual, rather than as the person known simply as "Mother" in her younger years. Now a mature woman herself, Shay could appreciate qualities in her mother that she'd never seen as a girl.

Watching her unobtrusively, Shay remembered how thin and tired and bitter Phyllis had been four years ago, still grieving over the meaningless death of her beloved Aaron at the hands of a drunken driver. Shay had devised her own brand of therapy, keeping herself busy with the garage for fourteen hours a day and leaving the boys, then seven and nine, to work their energetic magic on their grandmother. In a remarkably short time, Phyllis had regained much of her good humor and some necessary weight, the sparkle had returned to her blue eyes, and she'd had her silver-frosted dark auburn hair trimmed to a cap of feathery curls. Now, at fifty-four, she was an extremely attractive woman with great energy and a youthful zest for life that endeared her to her grandsons.

Finally, Shay caught her mother's eye and asked quietly, "What's wrong?"

"Shay, dear, are you *sure* all this is necessary?" Phyllis's obvious agitation was quite out of character, and Shay's eyebrows arched questioningly. "It's been years since a hurricane has hit here. The last few that came this far north went right off out to sea or up to the coast of Canada. I can't believe you need—"

"Mother! Good heavens, you know better than to ignore a hurricane warning. You *do* remember that 1938 hurricane, don't you? There was practically no warning, and no one knew what to do. How many died in that? Hundreds. And even the ones in the fifties and sixties, when we did get warnings, caused millions of dollars of damage and killed I don't know how many people."

Shay's attention had been concentrated on her mother, but at the sound of gasps and exclamations from the boys, she looked across the table at them. They had both paled, and their excitement was becoming touched with fear. Kyle glanced at his brother for reassurance. Marcus, at thirteen, was very much aware of how much his eleven-year-old brother looked up to him, and Shay could see the older boy resolutely pushing down the fear, straightening his back, and lifting his chin determinedly. Her eyes glowed with pride as she watched Kyle follow his brother's lead.

Shay turned back to her mother and paused with her mouth half-open, wondering what had brought a flush to her face and caused her eyes to go all dreamy. "What's the matter, Mother?"

"Umm? Oh! Nothing, nothing. I just . . . I was thinking about something." Looking totally flustered, Phyllis scrambled up and started clearing the table. "Well, don't just dawdle, children," she said briskly, including all three. "We've evidently got a lot to do in a short time. I'm just going to stack these dishes for now. It seems to me, Shay, that we should concentrate on the outside and barn first, while you're here. The boys and I can take care of everything in the house later. We should have plenty of time. We'll get a few hours' warning if the storm swings this way, won't we?"

"At least three or four, I should think," said Shay thoughtfully. She glanced at the clock and continued, "It's seven-fifteen now. We're late opening the station, and I think one of us should get over there. A lot of people are going to want to fill up both their cars and spare cans in case we lose power and can't pump gas. Mother, why don't you do that? You know how to run the pumps. Just do gas. If they want anything else, tell them to come back after ten."

"All right, dear, if you think that's best, but—"

"I don't want you doing any heavy lifting, Mother, and the main work around here is going to be getting in that porch furniture and collecting the wrought iron pieces from the lawns."

"Oh, dear, you're not going to try to carry those, are you?"

"No. We'll hook that small dolly onto the back of the mini-tractor and haul them up to the barn. Where do you want the porch furniture? Is there space in the sunroom, or shall we take it out to the barn?"

Phyllis was busy tucking her jeans into knee-high rubber boots, and her voice was muffled as she answered, "There should be plenty of room in the sunroom. What about those windows? Do you think they'll hold?"

"I think so. Dad got steel rather than aluminum frames, and the screens and the glass louvers should give enough to keep from blowing out. What about the vegetable garden? Even if we don't get the full storm, this mess is going to get worse, and there won't be much left out there by this afternoon."

"Oh, Lord, yes. I forgot about that. Well, first things first. Get everything secured, and then, if there's time, you could try to gather up as many tomatoes and cucumbers as possible. Even if they're not quite ripe, I can pickle them. And there's probably some more corn, maybe try to salvage the squash—it's a bit young, but we can do something with it. Seems a shame to let it blow away."

Phyllis was chattering nervously, and Shay put a reassuring hand on her shoulder, smoothing the collar of the bright yellow slicker as Phyllis fumbled with the catches. "We're going to be fine, Mother. Don't worry. This house has stood through everything for over a hundred years. We may lose some trees and the gardens and perhaps a few shingles, but the house isn't going to come down around our ears."

From the corner of her eye, Shay saw the boys coming from the back hall, which was in reality a small, stone-floored room used for everything from potting plants to storing fishing tackle. "Oh, no, not your slickers. They'll be too awkward. Wear your rain pants and jackets and your high boots. And use both the drawstrings and snaps on your hoods. That wind's building up. Look out there—the rain's almost horizontal."

"Okay, Mom," they chorused resignedly, shrugging out of their slickers and heading back to the long row of coat hooks lining one side of the hall.

"I really ought to get going, Shay. Where's the cash bag? I guess maybe I'll take my car, even for that short way."

Shay pulled open the warming drawer under the oven and extracted a small canvas money bag stamped with "Amherst National Bank" in fading black letters. "Here you are. Better take the Wagoneer. I filled your tank yesterday morning, but mine's down over a half. We should have them both full."

"Yes, of course. That's a good idea, isn't it?"

Shay frowned. It wasn't like her mother to make inane remarks or, for that matter, to dither as she'd been doing since breakfast. "Is something bothering you, Mother? I wouldn't have thought even a possible hurricane would make you this nervous. You're usually so calm and controlled, except," she added with a grin, "when you're bent on match-making."

Taking in her mother's suddenly guilty expression, Shay groaned, "Oh, no. *Now* what have you done?"

"I . . . uh . . . I just invited that nice man to lunch," Phyllis stammered, backing away from the forbidding expression on her daughter's face and edging toward the hall. "You did like him, dear, didn't you? He and the boys certainly hit it off. And the poor man doesn't get much chance for a good, home-cooked meal, living in that inn the way he does. I just thought . . ." Her voice trailed off and she made a dash for the back door, calling over her shoulder, "Be careful, dear. I'll see you later. Don't worry about a thing."

During the following hour or so, Shay didn't have time to worry about "that nice man," since she had too many more immediate problems. The rose garden, with its graveled paths and charming arbor, was Phyllis's pride and joy, and she had embellished it with graceful wrought iron seats and small tables. Unfortunately, although they looked delicate, they were very heavy. The rose garden was also at the far side of an acre of lawn, and it took longer than Shay had planned to move all of the pieces into the barn.

She had decided to work from the outer limits of the yard, in toward the house, finishing up with the porch furniture. From the rose garden, they moved on to the curved seats ringing the big white oak tree, which provided welcome shade near the croquet course in the side yard. Shay was becoming concerned about the boys. It wasn't just the weight of the furniture; they were also struggling against blasting gusts of wind that staggered them and drove the cold rain against their faces, making it hard to see. The increasingly soggy ground was also slowing them down, since it was difficult for the small tractor, usually used for mowing the acre and a half of lawn, to pull the heavily laden dolly across the sodden grass.

"Kyle, pull the tractor over onto the gravel path. Marcus

and I can carry the seats that far. Damn! Only two at a time will fit. We'll have to do it in two trips."

"Ow!"

"What is it?" called Shay, looking from one boy to the other.

"Piece of a limb blew down and hit me," yelled Kyle above the sound of the wind and rain. "It's okay. It wasn't very big."

"Move farther away from the tree," Shay yelled back. "Ready?" she asked Marcus. "Okay, let's go. God, these things weigh a ton," she gasped.

"Are you . . . sure we . . . couldn't leave . . . them here?" Marcus grunted.

They heaved the seat up onto the dolly, and Shay straightened up, stretching her back muscles and catching her breath. "Whooo. Only two more of those. No, Marcus, we can't leave them. A hundred-twenty-mile-an-hour wind, which is what's in that hurricane, could pick these seats up and drive them right through the side of the house. It's true," she assured him when she saw his disbelieving look. "Okay, Kyle, take it slow and easy up to the barn. Stay on the path. Marcus and I are going to bring the last two seats over here, ready for the next trip, and then we'll be up to unload."

Shay dropped an arm across her tall son's shoulders as they walked back under the tree. "What do you think, carrot curls, should we take a short break after we get these in, and get a hot drink? I'm freezing, and Kyle's looking a bit pinched around the edges."

"I could go for that."

"I'd forgotten how heavy these things were," Shay said as she worked her cold fingers around for a good grip on the edge of the next seat. "Maybe we should have borrowed a couple of McCormicks to give us a hand."

Marcus laughed as Shay described the ease with which the four McCormick boys, who were the size of linebackers, could probably stroll across the lawn with wrought iron seats dangling from each hand.

Between the howling of the storm and the muffling effect of her tightly fastened hood, Shay couldn't even hear the tractor, never mind a car on the far side of the house. But she did hear the deep male bellow that all but drowned out the roaring of the wind, startling her so that she almost dropped the heavy seat on her foot.

"You benighted, idiotic, lame-brained female! What in the blazing blue hell do you think you're doing?"

Still holding the seat, Shay and Marcus stared open-mouthed at the tall, furious man striding toward them, a bright green slicker flapping around the tops of his high boots, his platinum hair plastered to his head.

"Put that damn thing down!" he yelled, stopping in front of them.

Hastily, Shay and Marcus set the seat down on the ground. She turned back to the puzzlingly angry man and, deciding that she'd better try to soothe the savage beast, said placatingly, "Dag! What a surprise to see you here. What are you—"

"Are you out of your tiny mind?" demanded an obviously unsoothed Dag. He grabbed Shay by the shoulders and practically lifted her off her feet. "What is it with you, woman? Do you get a group rate for hernias? Is someone offering a package deal for more than two ruptured discs in a family? Pneumonia isn't so bad if you share it? Of all the stupid, half-witted, obstinate, idi—OW!"

Shay, getting madder by the second, had bypassed soothing and proceeded to direct action with a hard kick to Dag's left shin. He promptly dropped her and ostentatiously limped in a circle, moaning in agony. Marcus, off to one side, clapped his hands over his mouth to stifle a giggle.

"Oh, stop that," Shay growled disgustedly. "I couldn't possibly have hurt you with rubber boots, you great lump." She turned toward the iron seat. "Well, we haven't got time to visit right now. There's still a—"

"You touch that and I'll break your arm," Dag yelled, catching her wrist and swinging her away from the seat. "Pea-brain! I swear you've got a case of terminal stubbornness. Now take the boys inside and get the bunch of you warmed up before you're all sick."

"Don't be ridiculous!" Shay yelled right back, trying unsuccessfully to get her wrist loose. At the moment she was not in the least bit cold; she was blazing with temper. "I'm perfectly all right! I'm as healthy as a horse!"

"And horses are the dumbest animals in creation!" snarled

Dag, showing every indication of having a true MacAllister-style temper on his own.

The lid blew off. "And you are a horse's a—"

A hard yank on her wrist brought Shay crashing into the solid wall of Dag's chest, knocking the breath out of her and stunning her long enough for him to clamp long arms tightly around her, pinning her arms to her sides. He closed one huge hand around her head, preventing her instinctive attempt to evade his hard, punishing mouth as it crushed her half-parted lips and effectively smothered the rest of her unflattering description.

Shay heard a roaring in her ears and didn't know if it was from the wind or a lack of oxygen. Between the rib-crushing hold of Dag's arms and the smothering effect of his angry, rigid tongue filling her mouth, she couldn't seem to get her breath back. Struggling feebly against his strength, she wondered hazily if he had any idea how much power he was using against her. She couldn't think straight, and her confusion was only multiplied by the distant awareness that her body was still responding to the sexual pull of that damn rampaging Viking. With only her toes touching the ground, she couldn't brace herself to wrench away from him, and the tight binding of his arms was allowing no more than a weak fluttering of her hands.

Shay surrendered the fight and went limp in Dag's arms, letting his big body take her full weight. She almost ended up on the soggy ground, since he had simultaneously snapped out of his rage, evidently awakening to an awareness of what he was doing to her and immediately loosening his stranglehold. He promptly tightened his arms again as her knees buckled, but this time the arms were supportive rather than crushing.

Shocked brown eyes stared into equally shocked aqua-marine eyes.

Suddenly, they were jolted back to the reality of cold, wind-driven rain in their faces by the sound of the boys' uncertain, questioning voices.

"Mom?" "Dag?" "What's wrong?" "Are you mad at us, Dag?" "Mom, why do you look so funny?" "Did he hurt you?"

This last question from Marcus, his young voice cracking

with rising anger and worry, jerked Shay and Dag apart and brought them to a belated awareness of the side effects of two explosive tempers meeting head on.

"It's all right, Marcus," Shay said reassuringly, taking in the half-worried, half-determined look on his face and the surprisingly large fists clenched at his sides. With a mixture of wonder, dismay, and pride, she realized that he had been ready to take on a very large, physically fit, full-grown man in defense of her. Knowing how mortified he'd be if she did anything so mushy as hugging and kissing him in front of Dag, she limited herself to touching him gently on the cheek.

"Don't be upset, Marcus," Dag said apologetically, clearly more than a little upset himself and regretting the lack of control that might have lessened him in the boys' eyes.

Dag looked ruefully from one boy to the other. "I'm really sorry if I frightened you, but your mother," he stated with a man-to-man grin, "is enough to try the patience of a guru."

Shay's temper started to spark again, and she made a great show of stretching her arms and rolling her shoulders as she snapped, "If you're handing out apologies, one of them had better head this way. I'm the one with the bruised ribs and cramped muscles. I feel like I've just lost three out of three with a boa constrictor!"

Before Dag could pick up the gauntlet, Kyle finally managed to make himself heard. Eyeing his mother and Dag thoughtfully, he said, "You know, you sound just like Mr. and Mrs. McCormick. They're always yelling at each other, too, but the boys just say, 'There they go again.' And sometimes Mr. McCormick grabs Mrs. McCormick and kisses her, and the boys say, 'Whoops! They're at it again.' Once I saw—"

"Kyle . . ."

". . . Mr. McCormick pinch Mrs. McCormick on the bottom—"

"Kyle!"

". . . and she shook a rolling pin at him, and he said, 'Later, honey,' and went out the door laughing. I didn't understand it."

"I should hope not!" sputtered Shay. She turned to scowl

a chuckling Dag into silence and froze, her horrified eyes staring over his shoulder.

"Shay! What is it?" Dag exclaimed. He turned to look over his shoulder and sighed with relief. "For Pete's sake, Shay, from the look on your face, I thought Frankenstein was creeping up on me. Sorry, guys," he said to the two very large, very brawny young men standing a few feet behind him. "In all the . . . er . . . excitement, I forgot to introduce you. Crusher O'Neil and Dip Winslow; Shay MacAllister and Marcus and Kyle Severin."

"How do you do?" croaked Shay, wishing she could simply fade away like smoke in the wind. *They're huge! How could I not have seen them! Whatever must they be thinking? I'm going to murder that miserable beast!*

"Crusher and Dip are defensive tackles for UMass," Dag explained. "I figured from what Phyllis said that you could use some muscle power, so I asked them to lend a hand. They're working at the inn this summer on grounds maintenance."

Mercifully he drew the explanation out, giving Shay time to collect herself. Shay lifted her head and met his eyes. At the sight of the warm apology she read there, her tense muscles relaxed and the painful lump in her throat melted away.

My God! I was on the verge of tears. What is this man doing to me? I haven't cried in ten years.

Dag slid a protective arm around her shoulders and turned her toward the house. "Let's get moving before we all dissolve. Marcus, Kyle, you guys have done a terrific job, and I think you've more than earned a break. Why don't you run in and get warm, while King and Kong here help me finish hauling in the lawn furniture. Your mother will be right along as soon as she shows us what else needs to be done."

Dag started them moving along the path, but Marcus turned to look hesitantly at his mother. At her reassuring nod he visibly relaxed and started jogging toward the back door. Kyle, however, was fixed on the fascinating sight of Crusher and Dip each swinging one of the heavy iron seats onto his shoulder and striding easily across the grass toward the barn.

"Wow," Kyle breathed, staring after them. "Wish they'd been here an hour ago."

"They would have been," growled Dag, "if your mother hadn't raised pigheaded stubbornness to an art form."

Laughing, Kyle raced after his brother. Shay could feel Dag's eyes on her, and she carefully kept her expression bland and her gaze fixed on the back of her departing son.

"Somehow," she said musingly, "I seem to have lost control of this family. In less than twenty-four hours, you've come, you've seen, and you've taken over. And you wondered why I called you a Viking raider! The first chance I get, I'm going to find you a horned helmet."

Dag's grin was enough to incite a self-respecting Mac-Allister female to commit, at the least, mayhem. However, his mind was clearly fixed on grinding his own axe.

"I don't suppose," he said, guiding her steps across the lawn toward the barbeque patio, "that it ever occurred to you to call me this morning and ask for some help. Of course not, Lady Independence. You'd rather drag the boys out here in the middle of a howling gale and struggle with those damn chunks of iron, which are way too heavy for any of you, than to admit that maybe, just maybe, there's something you can't handle all by yourself. Thank heavens at least one member of this family has some of that famous Yankee common sense."

Neither of them spoke again until they reached the patio, and Shay turned to him to explain what had to be done.

She got as far as "All that—" when Dag muttered an unrepeatable expletive and pushed her behind a large rhododendron, which screened them from both the barn and the house.

"Dag! Now what's the matter?"

"Your mouth." With one arm around her shoulders, holding her close to him, he tipped her face up with his other hand. His expression as he met her eyes was contrite, and his voice sounded oddly shaken as he said, "I'm sorry, sweetheart. I never meant to hurt you. That looks so sore . . ."

His mouth touched hers gently and then lingered as their cold lips warmed with the contact. Cold, aching, drained from the explosive confrontation, Shay suddenly was filled with an overwhelming need for comfort, and without further thought she leaned against his strength, sliding her arms around his waist and opening her mouth to the soothing touch of his tongue on the bruised inner flesh of her lips.

I'm going to regret this once I have time to think about it. I should never have shown even a hint of weakness to him. Let him get one of his big feet in the door and he'll take over my whole life. Until something more interesting comes along. Oh, hell!

For long moments, they were unaware of the rain beating down on them and the strong gusts of wind flinging wet leaves and twigs against them. It wasn't until a forgotten pot of ivy geraniums crashed to the patio floor that they came back to the wet, wind-whipped present.

"Go along in, sweetheart, and get warmed up. It shouldn't take the three of us long to finish up out here. You might make a pot of coffee, and those two behemoths will probably be hungry again; they seem to eat every two or three hours."

"Okay," said Shay with remarkable meekness. *I must be tireder than I thought.*

She told him what furniture went where, started for the piazza, intending to go in through the sunroom, and then hesitated and turned as a couple of Dag's remarks came back to her.

"Did my mother call you?"

"Of course. As I said, one member of the family has sense. Go on in, Shay. We'll discuss your other harebrained plans in a while."

She glared at him but bit back her instinctive rejoinder and continued toward the piazza, fuming every step of the way. *Harebrained. I'll show you harebrained, you Norse menace. You have nothing to do with my plans. If you have your way, I'll probably end up in a rocking chair, wrapped in a shawl, with a hot brick at my feet. Chauvinist! Caveman! You should be wearing a bearskin. Bare skin. Ummm...oh, Shay, you're losing your mind.*

chapter 5

THE BIG KITCHEN was pleasantly warm with the heat generated from the fire in the huge old black iron stove. Knowing the vagaries of the village's electricity in high winds, Phyllis had kept the antique over the years to supplement the electric stove and to provide at least one warm, dry place in the house during storms. The power had gone out an hour before. With the soft glow of the oil lamps and the tantalizing aromas from the large pot of stew simmering at the back of the old range and the apple pies baking in its oven, the kitchen seemed a safe haven from the violence of the storm raging outside.

Turning a deaf ear to Shay's halfhearted protests, Dag, Crusher, and Dip had not only secured the house and barn, but had also descended on the garage. Despite what she tried to tell herself about overbearing, pushy men, Shay was honest enough to admit to herself that it was a relief not to have to cope with all the heavy work with just the boys' help. Not that she was going to tell Dag that. Nor was she going to let him see any of the confusion he'd thrown her into by his actions that morning. She wished there was time for her to sit down quietly, and alone, to think through the whole situation. That, however, was impossible. There was just too much happening.

Once the MacAllisters were secure, Dag and his cohorts had lent their muscle power to several of the elderly villagers who had no one to help them prepare for the storm. At one point Shay had watched the three of them loping across the Green and had bemusedly wondered how she'd acquired such an unlikely trio of guardian angels.

She and Dag had managed to avoid any further confrontations during the afternoon, mainly because they hadn't been together for more than a few minutes at a time. He'd been busy on the other side of the village when she had received a series of road calls, so he hadn't been able to object to her going out with the truck alone. However, he'd had a few pithy comments to make when he found out about it afterward. With Phyllis, the boys, Crusher, and Dip present, he'd confined himself to scowling at her ferociously when she'd come in, shivering and exhausted-looking, from the last call.

Although it wasn't even five-thirty, outside the sky was dark with the heavy, swirling storm clouds. Kyle turned up the radio, and they all listened in dismay to the Weather Bureau spokesman announcing that the hurricane had intensified, changed course, and picked up forward speed. As of five-fifteen, it was moving at approximately sixty miles an hour straight for the southeastern Massachusetts coast. The winds in the storm had been clocked at 165 miles an hour, and it was moving on a 140-mile front. The leading edge was expected to hit the coast shortly after eight-thirty that evening. If it held to its present course, the eye of the storm would pass over Boston, northeastern Massachusetts, southeastern New Hampshire, and into southern Maine. The perimeter would reach as far inland as the central portions of Connecticut and Massachusetts and most of southern New Hampshire.

"Oh, hell! I'll have to get ready to head in to the Barracks," Shay muttered, walking over to the range and holding her hands out to warm them. With the vital part of the announcement over, talk broke out around the table.

"They didn't think it was going to swing this far west. It really changed course with a vengeance."

"Is it going to hit here? Right here?"

"Looks like it, Kyle."

"Will the roof blow away?"

"Of course not. This roof has survived any number of hurricanes and winter blizzards. We'll be all right."

"What about the windows? Will they blow in?"

"No! At least, not unless something hits them."

"Can I go with you, Mom?"

"Certainly not! I need you to stay here and take care of Nana and Kyle."

"Aw, Mom, I can take care of myself."

"Crusher and Dip will be here, Marcus. I'm going with your mother."

"No, you're not. Excuse me, folks, but I've got to eat and get moving."

Shay filled a bowl with stew and sat down across from Dag. She concentrated on the hot, filling stew while Dag explained, in what he evidently considered a reasonable tone of voice, why he was not going to let her go alone.

"You are utterly mad," said Shay firmly. "You are most certainly not going with me. I don't need a keeper, thank you. I know perfectly well what I'm doing, and—"

"If you think for one moment I'm going to allow you to go romping off into the middle of a hurricane all by yourself, you can forget it! Talk about mad! The whole thing is crazy!" Dag slammed both hands down on the sturdy oak kitchen table and leaned forward to glare at Shay.

Pushing back her chair, Shay stood up, jammed her fists against her hips, and glared back at Dag. "It isn't going to do you a bit of good to yell at me, and—"

"I'm not yelling!"

". . . and slamming the table—"

"I did not slam the table!"

". . . isn't going to get you anywhere, either."

"You are not going out of here without me!"

"You just watch me!"

The five people still seated at the table looked like spectators at a tennis match as they turned from the tall, obstinate woman to the taller, frustrated man, and back again. A sigh that sounded suspiciously like disappointment went around the table when the ringing of the phone cut short what was shaping up to be another fascinating confrontation.

"MacAllister's," snapped Shay, grabbing the phone.

She recognized Tony Clinton from his chuckle even before he spoke. "Bad day, Shay? Save your temper, honey, it's going to be a worse night."

"So I just heard. Lord knows it's bad enough out there now. I came down by Sime's Brook three-quarters of an hour ago, and it's starting to overflow. If it gets much higher, it's going to flood the road."

"Some places are already flooded. We've got a lot of power and phone lines down, too. I wasn't sure I'd be able to get you. Some of these wind gusts are topping seventy, and there are already trees and large limbs coming down on the roads. Better get on in here as soon as you can. It's going to be a bitch."

"We're still going to get it, even this far west?"

"As of now, we're expecting the outer edge, and that's packing winds up to a hundred and twenty miles an hour, which is going to be plenty bad enough. If it shifts just a bit farther west we'll really get slammed. Listen, Shay, we're going to need all the muscle we can get once we're back on the roads. Do you think you could bring one of the McCormick boys with you?"

Shay turned toward Dag, who was standing in the middle of the kitchen with his arms folded across his wide chest, looking like the original immovable object. With a sardonic grin, she said, "Never mind a McCormick. I've got six and a half feet of muscle right here just itching to get in on the action. We'll be on our way in another ten or fifteen minutes. See you."

"Wait, Shay!"

"What?"

"If you've got a power saw, bring it along."

"What are—"

"Everyone's going to be spread out. We won't always be able to wait for a highway crew to clear trees and limbs off smashed cars."

"Makes sense. Do you need more saws? I'm pretty sure Ev Stoner has at least a few in stock, and I know he'll lend them. Want me to call him?"

"If you would. We can pay a rental fee for them."

"Okay. See you shortly."

Shay hung up and turned back to Dag, only to find him

disappearing up the back stairs at her mother's heels. From the snatches of conversation drifting back, she realized that Phyllis was planning to outfit him with warmer clothes. Shay remembered that her mother had stored all her father's things rather than give them away, and her father had been close to Dag's size.

"Want me to get the power saw? That's what you were talking about, isn't it?"

Marcus's voice brought Shay's attention back to her own problems. She saw the worry on his face and knew he'd feel better if he could help. "Yes, and it would save us a few minutes if you could get it. Do you know where it is?"

"In the garage under the barn. Where shall I put it—in the back of the truck?"

"On the floor in front," Shay called over her shoulder as she headed for the stairs. "It'll get soaked in back."

Leaping up the stairs two at a time, Shay tried to remember where she'd stored her thermal longjohns. It was going to be a long, cold, raw night, and once the worst of the hurricane had passed, she was going to be spending hours outdoors in wind and rain. Her rain pants and jacket would keep her reasonably dry, but they weren't very warm.

Twenty minutes later, Shay and Dag were ready to leave. They were warmly dressed in flannel-lined jeans over thermal longjohns, long-sleeved cotton-knit jerseys, and ski sweaters, and they'd pulled on double pairs of heavy socks to wear under the waterproofed leather boots that were laced up to their knees.

Marcus and Kyle had been listening to the hurricane reports on the radio while Shay and Dag got ready. The bulletins had been interspersed with stories of previous hurricanes, and the boys were now white-faced and tight-lipped as they realized that what had seemed like an exciting adventure that morning was actually a frightening and dangerous experience.

Both boys had their arms wrapped tightly around their mother, and Shay hugged them close, trying to reassure them.

"Mama," Kyle choked, trying not to cry, "what if you get hurt?"

"Can't Crusher or Dip go with Dag? Do you have to

go?" asked Marcus, looking at her with wide, worried eyes.

Too upset to realize the implications of what she was doing, Shay instinctively looked at Dag in appeal.

"Have a heart, guys," said Dag. "None of us knows the first thing about handling a tow truck. There's got to be at least one expert along. We're probably going to have some nasty messes to sort out, and your mother's the only one with real know-how."

With a hand on each boy's shoulder he swung them around to face him. He looked intently from one to the other, his face set in a hard, confident expression. "I promise you I'll take good care of your mother. I won't let her get hurt. Don't forget, she's been doing this for a long time, and she's very good at it. She doesn't take silly chances. Okay?"

"Okay," said Kyle, looking more like his normal self. "As long as you're going to be with her, we won't worry."

"Besides," said Marcus, "I just remembered. Mom's an advanced EMT, and they'll need her for that, too."

Dag waited until they were backing out of the drive to satisfy his curiosity. "You're a qualified EMT? Emergency Medical Technician?"

"Right," said Shay, turning left on Center Village Road, which circled the Green. "Ev Stoner, Dan McCormick, and I took the same course ambulance attendants and fire fighters take. This is a small village. We're nine miles from the nearest doctor, eleven miles from the nearest ambulance, and fourteen miles from a hospital. With three EMT's living in the center of the village, there's bound to be at least one of us available in an emergency. In my case, it's particularly useful, because I often get to the scene of an accident well before the ambulance."

"Makes sense. Guess I'm not used to the self-sufficiency of country villages. Why are you stopping at the store? Isn't it closed?"

"Ev Stoner's lending the State Police some power saws. I called him while I was getting dressed, and he's meeting us here. Ah, there he is. Practically getting blown off his feet. Let's go."

It took real effort to open the cab doors against the powerful gusts of wind, and once they were outside, the driving rain half blinded them. Ev Stoner, a slightly built man in his fifties, was staggering under the impact of the wind, and Shay and Dag closed in on both sides of him to shield him while he unlocked the store.

Working quickly, Shay and Dag loaded several new power saws, still in their individual heavy-duty shipping cartons, into the back of the truck, fitting them around the base of the hoisting rig. Shay had filled several two- and five-gallon gas cans earlier, and now she clamped them securely into place.

"Don't like gas cans rattling around," she said, wiping the rain from her face after they climbed back into the cab and starting the truck. "They should be safe enough now unless we turn over."

Dag looked at her with raised brows. "Wouldn't think these things would flip very easily."

"They don't," she said, laughing. "You wouldn't believe how heavily weighted these rigs are. Well, you may find out before the night's over. Okay, here we go. I'm going to try the Amherst Road. It's the widest and least likely to be blocked. Look over there. There's already some big stuff coming down."

Shay could feel sweat trickling down her spine and knew it was from nerves. Her shoulders were starting to ache, and she consciously forced her muscles to relax. Although she had to use some muscle power to hold the truck on the road against the gale-force gusts of wind, she knew that most of her tension and strain was due to the effort of trying to see. Even with high beams on, the wipers at their fastest speed, and crawling at less than twenty miles an hour, she was still finding it almost impossible to stay on the road.

She didn't dare take her eyes from the road, but she was very much aware of Dag watching her. Remembering the indications of his protectiveness throughout the day, especially his surprising anger that morning when he'd found her struggling with the wrought iron, she wondered if he was going to try to insist on driving. She hoped not. This was no time for futile arguments. No matter how it might dent his male pride, he was just going to have to accept that this was something she could do and he couldn't. He simply didn't know the road well enough to drive it in near-zero visibility.

Anticipating an argument at any moment and wondering why he was holding back, she started to tense up again. When she heard him swear under his breath, her immediate reaction was: *Here we go again!*

It was a shock, therefore, to hear the frustration in his voice when he said, "I wish there were some way I could help you. I feel so damn useless."

"Oh, but you're not!" she exclaimed. "It's a help just having you here. But what you can do is try to see the road on your side. Let me know if you think I might be getting too far over, or if you see anything that looks like a tree or a car or whatever. Do you have your watch?"

"Yeah." He leaned forward, pushing back the cuff of his sweater and turning his wrist toward the dash light. "It's ten of seven."

"Better switch on the radio so we can keep up with the weather."

They didn't speak again for some time, both of them concentrating on trying to see ahead of the truck. The seven o'clock news was all bad. Wind gusts of up to a hundred miles an hour were hitting the coastal areas in advance of the hurricane, and hundreds of boats had already been damaged, beached, or sunk. Two people were missing from a marina on the Cape, and the shorelines on Nantucket, Martha's Vineyard, and Cape Cod were being pounded by fifteen- to twenty-foot seas. Worst of all, the hurricane was apparently veering slightly to the northwest, which would bring more of it over heavily populated land areas.

Shay and Dag swore softly. There was nothing else worth saying.

Peering intently through the windshield a few minutes later, Dag asked, "Is there any significance to a white fence on this side, maybe ten feet back from the road?"

"Hell, yes," Shay exclaimed, slowing to an inching crawl. "We're coming to the intersection with Borley Road. Keep your eyes peeled. There's a brook that comes down along the other side of Borley, and it might be over its banks."

"Watch it! I think that's more than rain right ahead. See it?"

Shay braked gently to a stop and let the truck idle in neutral. She took a few seconds to flex her cramped fingers and then reached for the spotlight handle. With the truck at a standstill, the wipers gave slightly better visibility, and perhaps the spot would now serve a useful purpose. Shay played it slowly over the road in front of them and picked up the unmistakable glitter of swiftly running water.

"Damn, damn," she breathed, directing the light across the intersection, trying to pick up roadside features to judge how deep the flow was.

"Do you want me to walk ahead of you?" Dag asked quietly.

"I don't—Ah, there. See? That rock over there," said Shay, steadying the light. "I don't think there's much more than a foot of water, and we can get through that okay."

Aiming the spotlight at a point several feet in front of the truck, she locked it into place, shifted into low gear, and started inching through the water. From that point on, their way was reasonably clear aside from the two places where they had to ease around downed trees partially blocking the road. They saw no other vehicles until they reached the intersection with Route 9, and even after turning onto the highway they found very little traffic.

"Looks like most people are being sensible and listening to the warnings," Dag said, the first words either of them had spoken in twenty minutes. "How are you doing?"

"A whole lot better now that we're off that damn black road. It was like driving blind through a tunnel. Not that it's any easier to see through this downpour, but at least this road has white lines, and I can stop worrying about putting us into a ditch."

She reached out to flip the switch activating the orange flashers mounted on the hoisting rig. "Better let the world know what we are. Keep a sharp watch on that side, Dag, in case of stalled cars. We'll have to check them out for anyone stranded."

"Right." Peering into the unbroken darkness on both sides of the wide road, he murmured, "It's hard to believe this stretch of Route 9 is lined with gas stations, eating places, and shops. The power must be out in this whole sector."

"I swear it's raining even harder, or else the wind's stronger. Can't get a glimmer of any of the emergency lighting in these motels and restaurants. It's battery powered, so it must be on."

"It's like—Flashing blue and red lights up ahead," Dag said urgently. "See them? On this side."

"Got it. Looks like a Statie."

Shay slowed and eased to the right, stopping behind the two-tone blue State Police cruiser. She checked Dag as he reached for the door handle. "Why don't you wait here for a minute? No sense both of us getting wet. I'll call you if I need help." She opened her door and slid out, laughing back at his muttered, "Female chauvinist!"

The force of the wind took her breath away and pushed her against the side of the truck. Staggering in a half-crouch, her head tucked down against the whipping rain, she groped along the high fender and then lunged across the open space between the truck and cruiser, crashing head-on into a solid body. Hands caught her arms and swung her around against the side of the cruiser, the big figure moving close to shield her from the worst of the wind. Squinting against the glare of the truck's headlights, Shay peered into the face under the stiff brim of the uniform cap.

"Brady? Good thing you aren't Martinson; I'd have flattened you." She grinned at the brawny trooper, picturing a very different result if she'd slammed into the much smaller Martinson. "You need any help?"

"Not with this one," he said, returning her smile and waving a hand toward the sedan parked in front of the cruiser. "Are you on a call or heading in to the Barracks?"

"On my way in. How much longer are you going to be on the road? It's getting impossible to see, and stuff's beginning to fly through the air," Shay gasped as she instinctively ducked to avoid getting smacked in the face with a cluster of wet leaves.

"We're all heading in that direction now. Come on, I'll help you get back." With a bracing arm around her, Brady turned Shay and started walking toward the truck. "We're checking out any cars stopped along the road to make sure everyone's out of them. You wouldn't believe how dumb some people are. I found one family of four in a Volks, and the guy explained that they'd stopped because the wind was pushing them all over the road and he figured they'd be safer if they parked until the storm was over."

Shay paused with her hand on the door latch, looking at Brady disbelievingly. "What the hell did he think was going to happen to a Volks in a hundred-seventy-something mile wind?"

"Nothing," said Brady disgustedly. "It took me five minutes to get it through his head that that car was going to flip around like a marble in a pinball machine. At that, it was his wife who finally insisted that she and the kids at least were going to a safe place. He decided to go with them."

"Crazy," Shay muttered as she pulled open the door with some help from the big trooper. When she started to introduce him to Dag, she discovered that they'd already met.

"Rotten night, Dag," said Brady. "The cleanup's going to be ugly. I'm glad Shay's going to have you with her. Listen, babe," he said to Shay as he gave her a hand into the driver's seat, "we might as well stick together the rest of the way in. I may need you to shove abandoned cars out of the travel lanes. Okay?"

"Sure. We'll be right on your tail."

Moving slowly, their mingled blue, red, and orange flashing lights reflecting off the cascading rain in an eerily festive glow, the police car and the tow truck proceeded in a halting progression down the highway. They were stopped several times by motorists who had left it to the last minute to find shelter, and who now, unfamiliar with the area and unable to see anything with the power out, could not locate a motel or an emergency shelter. Occasionally they slowed beside a parked car, using their spotlights to check for occupants, and Brady acquired three human passengers and a dog.

"What's he doing?" Shay muttered as the cruiser moved to the middle of the road and its brake lights came on.

"Something's in this lane," said Dag, leaning forward to try to see better. "I think it's a car side-on."

Shay eased up beside the cruiser and rolled her window down partway. Brady, leaning across the front seat, yelled up at her, "Push it to the side. I'm going to take these people to the shelter. I'll be back."

She gave him a thumbs-up and rolled her window shut. Wiping the rain from her face with one hand, she reached under the seat with the other and handed Dag a tire iron. "You're going to have to steer that car while I push. If the door's locked, break the side window. We don't have time to fool around."

Dag didn't waste any of that time, either. His only comment as he went out the door was a laughing, "The insurance companies must love you."

"I couldn't see anything out there," he said once he was back in the truck and they were on their way again. "Do you know where we are?"

"Roughly," Shay answered, glancing at him quickly. "You've got leaves stuck all over you. What was that that blew across in front of you?"

"A wooden box or a chest, I think. There're some shingles flying around out there, too, and some small tree limbs."

"We're almost to the Barracks. Maybe another five minutes if we don't have to stop again." She couldn't hide the huskiness in her voice, and Dag turned to look at her. She knew a muscle was twitching along her jawline; she was tensing up over the last weather bulletin. The hurricane had swung even farther in their direction. It was now over Nantucket and Martha's Vineyard, and fragmented radio transmissions from the islands indicated widespread damage from both the powerful winds and the extraordinarily high seas.

Dag quietly reached over and laid his hand along her cheek. "Shay?"

"I'm okay." In a sudden overwhelming need for comfort, she pressed her face against his hand and swallowed hard. "It's going to be even worse than we thought," she said, and there was a mixture of anguish and dread in her voice.

From the corner of her eye she saw him turn quickly toward her, and then she felt his hand slide down across her shoulder and arm, finally coming to rest on her thigh. The warm weight of it was reassuring, and she sensed that he, like she, was thinking about the morning hours, after the storm had passed, when they would be part of the disaster crews clearing the roads and, inevitably, searching for and finding those, both dead and injured, who had not escaped nature's rage. Some of it would be sickening; some of it would be ugly; all of it would be tragic.

Shay saw the blue and red flashers coming toward her

and stopped to wait for Brady to turn. In those few moments, she turned her head to look at Dag and met the compassion and understanding clearly showing in his eyes. She dropped her hand to cover his, and their fingers intertwined tightly as they held each other's gaze in a silent dialogue, sharing their strength and courage.

"It's going to be terrible," she finally whispered. "People will die."

"Yes, but I'll be with you and help you every way I can."

She let out a long sighing breath and squeezed his hand hard. "I know you will."

Her belief in him was as strong as it was inexplicable. She closed her eyes momentarily, wondering what there was about this man that compelled her to trust him. Somehow, in just over twenty-four hours, he had managed to chip away at her cherished independence without her even realizing he was doing it. Still, she reminded herself, he was just a man, and she couldn't afford to rely too heavily on him. The memories of Cary's unreliability and fickleness went deep, and she was determined never again to hand over the responsibility for her own and her sons' well-being to a man. Not even this one.

But she couldn't quite still the voice of her personal gremlin whispering: *Are you sure? Remember, there's an exception to every rule. Maybe, just maybe, he's your exception.*

chapter 6

SHAY SLEPT THROUGH the hurricane.

For years afterwards, it was one of the favorite Shay-stories among her family and friends. Phyllis MacAllister's response when she heard about it said it all: "Heavens, dear, I know I've always said you could sleep through anything, but good grief, Shay! *A hurricane?*"

Shay's explanation was always a laughing, "I couldn't help it. It'd been a long, tense day, and I was tired. The damn storm had slowed down when it hit land, and we were going to be sitting around and waiting for three or four hours. Besides, Dag's shoulder was soooo comfortable."

She never added the information that she'd had no intention of falling asleep. By the time she and Dag trailed Brady into the Barracks day room, her attention was only partly on the activity taking place around her. The rest of her mind was wrestling with those inexplicable moments in the truck. She couldn't understand the sudden need that had welled up from somewhere deep inside her; a need for comfort, for reinforcement of her own strength. How had she dared let him see that at that moment she needed to lean just a little on his strength? How could she have been so sure that he wouldn't see it as a sign of weakness, a breach in her protective walls through which he could gain the advantage over her? What had happened to her rock-hard determination never to depend on a man again? Oh, yes, she was depending on him. It was all there in that handclasp and the long exchange of . . . what?

There had been so much in that intense locking of eyes. Yesterday afternoon he had come on like the original macho man, but since then, almost hour by hour, she had sensed the deepening of his interest and understanding. She had also discovered some unexpected things about him.

His protectiveness had surprised her. Very few men felt it necessary to protect an Amazon. That's why she had been so slow to comprehend his anger that morning and had kept right on lifting that seat. She'd never been so shocked in her life as when he'd thrown a royal temper fit. She was going to have bruises for a week. He certainly did have strong hands—probably from years of playing basketball. He had a strong character, too, which was another surprise. No, the surprise was in the depth of character and in the dimensions of his self-confidence. It was apparent, now, that he wasn't at all macho; he had no need to flaunt his masculinity to prove that it was there. He didn't see tenderness and compassion as weaknesses. His maleness was such an integral part of him, his confidence in his masculinity so bone-deep, that nothing could threaten it—not even a stubbornly independent, contrary Amazon with a testy temper.

He thought her temper was amusing. Well, except for this morning. But he was already mad as hell when she blew up then. Usually, he laughed at her. What could you do with a man like that? Hang onto him? Maybe. The boys liked him. Phyllis liked him. Despite herself, she liked him. All right, she more than liked him. The sexual attraction between them wasn't to be believed, and it was definitely mutual. That mini-explosion last night on the veranda had shaken them both. It's a wonder they hadn't ended up on the floor.

"Shay, do you want some coffee?"

Dag's insistent voice brought her back to the day room, and she blinked at him as her mind groped to catch up with the present. She murmured, "Please," and glanced around the room as he headed for the coffee urn. Everywhere she looked she saw blue. She knew all the troopers stationed at the Barracks, and it looked as if most of them were here, lounging around the big room, drinking coffee and exchanging stories of their last few hours' experiences. The physical fitness requirements for troopers were stringent, and seeing so many of them together, Shay was impressed with what a rugged-looking group they were in their distinctive uniforms of medium-blue shirts, dark-blue cavalry-style pants with a lighter blue stripe down the sides, and heavy, black leather knee-high boots.

She decided after a moment or two that at least part of her mind must have been functioning on auto-pilot. She had evidently greeted most of the troopers, introduced Dag to several of them, and—as she realized suddenly—discovered that he already knew many of them. Well, that figured. A lot of guys were sports fans, and he'd been in the area for several months, so...

"Milk and one sugar. Right?" Dag asked, handing her a styrofoam cup.

"Terrific. I need this. How come you know so many of these guys?"

"Met a few here and there, and they introduced me to others. Some of them are volunteer coaches with various kids' sports programs. Dan knows most of the men stationed here, and he introduced me to some. Good group."

Shay glanced around and found a number of amused eyes fixed on them, with several *knowing* grins directed at her, and she felt her face flushing.

Leaning closer to Dag, she whispered, "Why are they looking at us like that? As if... as if... I don't know. I get the feeling they know something I don't."

Dag half turned to screen her from most of the room, and smiled a slow, sensual smile as his eyes skimmed down her body. For the first time, Shay became aware that somewhere along the line they had removed their rain gear and boots and were padding around in their stocking feet. She looked at that smile, felt the warm bubbles rising in her stomach, and audibly gulped.

"Stop looking at me like that," she hissed. "No wonder they—"

"Steady, girl," Dag all but purred. "Let's grab that couch in the corner, and I'll explain the code to you."

"What code?" asked a frustrated Shay as she let him guide her to a small, two-person upholstered settee. They sat down, and Dag stretched out one long leg and hooked his toes under the edge of a narrow, unfinished pine coffee table, pulling it over so that they could both put their feet on it.

Shay sipped her coffee and asked again, "What code?"

Looking smugly amused, Dag murmured, "The one that men use to let each other know if a woman's taken, available, not worth the effort, possible, or in any one of several other categories." He slanted a look at her and chuckled at her outraged expression. "Are you grinding your teeth, love? Shouldn't do that. It's bad for the enamel."

"I don't believe you!" she snarled, barely managing to keep her voice below a yell and forcing herself to lean back and at least give the impression of being relaxed.

"Would I make that up?" Dag protested, widening his eyes innocently.

"Is that what you did? Gave them some kind of signal? Is that why they're giving us those Cheshire cat grins?" She turned her head and nailed him with a sizzling look. "What did you do?" she asked ominously.

He studied her for a moment and set his cup on the floor beside him. Plucking Shay's cup out of her hand and holding it beyond her reach, he smiled challengingly at her and said dulcetly, "I let them know you were all mine."

"You did *what?*" she yelled, leaping to her feet and towering over him, her fists planted on her slim hips. He lounged back comfortably and laughed up at her.

For a few seconds there was a startled silence in the room, and then several of the men chuckled, and one called out, "Hey, Norseman, are you sure you don't want to join up? We could use a guy with your guts." Another voice, filled with wonder, chimed in with, "Man's got nerves of steel. Lights her fuse and sits there laughing. I'd rather tease a tiger."

There was a rising chorus of male laughter. Although Shay knew her temper was legendary, she rarely blew up without just cause. However, in the course of working with her at many accident scenes over the past four years, many of the troopers had seen her verbally blow away busy bystanders who were interfering with rescue operations. It slowly dawned on her that they were all waiting with amused curiosity to see how Dag would handle her.

She spun around, her long heavy braid whipping over her shoulder to fall between her breasts. Her scorching gaze should have melted the bullets in their guns.

"Don't you all sit there grinning like a bunch of monkeys! Why don't you go—"

"Shay . . ." Dag's deep voice was a soft warning.

". . . out and play in the hurricane! Or polish your bullets and mind your own—"

"Shut up, sweetheart," Dag said mildly, grabbing her wrist and yanking her back down onto the couch. Before she could get her balance, he had one arm around her shoulders and had wound her braid around his other hand, pulling her head close to his. Aware of the interested audience, he dropped his voice to a whisper as he threatened, "You're very sexy when you're mad, and if you don't simmer down, I'm going to have to kiss you. And you know how you react to that!"

Shay glared at the teasing sherry eyes only scant inches from her own and hissed in frustration through her gritted teeth. Her left hand was clutching his wrist, trying to ease the pull on her hair, while her other hand was caught between his side and the back of the couch. She considered and reluctantly discarded several violent moves. Although there might be a fleeting satisfaction in biting a chunk out of his earlobe or punching him in the nose, she had no illusions about his letting her get away with it. Not after she'd had a sample of his temper that morning.

She watched him warily, but she was determined to have the last word. "Conceited beast!" she growled.

He glanced at her mouth and grinned at her jutting lower lip. "Pull it in, sweetness, or I won't be able to resist," he chided huskily.

She half opened her mouth, but then met the dare-you gleam in his eyes and subsided, the tautness going out of her body as she leaned her shoulder against the settee back. She was still held in the curve of his arm, but now he unwound her braid from around his hand and contented himself with toying with the curly end of it. For another long moment their eyes met in a measuring look, and then Shay threw her head back and laughed.

A relieved sigh went up from the watching troopers, who apparently hadn't known whether to set up the first-aid kit or clear the room. Under cover of the rising volume of talk and laughter, Dag muttered, "Close, very close. You do believe in living dangerously, love."

"So do you," she snapped. "You've got no right playing conquering male with me and telling them I'm yours. Whatever that's supposed to mean, I'm damn well not it. Really, Dag, you've got to get over this Viking syndrome of yours."

"Too late, I'm afraid," he sighed. "Now that I've picked out my own personal Valkyrie, I can't quit until I've convinced you to take the job."

"Whatever are you babbling about? Weren't Valkyries those big blond goddesses with braids to their knees and iron breastplates? It's a wonder they weren't humpbacked from the weight."

Dag choked on a mouthful of coffee and sputtered for a few seconds before he could gasp, "Oh, Lord, I can see them now! Where did you learn your mangled mythology? Pay attention now. Valkyries were the beautiful handmaidens of the god Odin, who were sent to collect the souls of slain warriors, bring them to Valhalla, and wait upon them hand and foot." He gave Shay an outrageously seductive smile and continued, "You have to admit that a brave warrior deserves all the pampering he can get."

Shay gave him a narrow-eyed look and said in measured tones, "You are not a warrior."

"But, sweetheart," he coaxed, "surely in these enlightened times we can consider an athlete a reasonable equivalent. Myths, like customs, have to adapt to progress, so I think being retired is a logical substitute for being slain. Slain is so final. I'm sure you wouldn't enjoy pampering a dead body."

Shay stared at him in open-mouthed disbelief. Finally she managed a strangled, "You're really quite mad! Your horns have ingrown, right through your helmet into your brain."

Obviously exerting monumental self-control, Dag managed not to laugh and conjured up a mournful expression that would have turned a bloodhound green with envy. "Are you trying to tell me that you don't want to be my Valkyrie?" He even managed to put a break in his voice.

Shay cast an appealing look at the ceiling. "Did I say there were no more original approaches? Was it my voice that said I'd heard every line invented by man?"

Dag tugged on her braid to bring her gaze back to his face. His expression was reassuring and his voice soothing. "It's not that difficult. I'm sure you'll catch on in no time at all. There's no need for you to feel inadequate just because you don't have snakey blond braids. I'll tell you—"

"Inadequate!"

". . . what we'll do. We'll give you a genuine Old Norse name. Shay the Fire-Haired. Couldn't be—"

"And you're Dag the Mush-Minded."

". . . more fitting. You'll be unique—the only red-haired Valkyrie in existence. No problem with your height, and you've definitely got a goddessy figure. Mmmm. Definitely. The only snag is those iron breastplates. I think—"

"You may be slain, yet."

". . . you're right—they're much too heavy. Probably chafe you, too. What about aluminum, or perhaps one of those lightweight alloys? And I don't think—"

"I think you were out in the wind too long."

". . . we should get the kind with points in the middle of the cups. I'd get all scratched up."

Shay gave up, closed her eyes, and let her head drop sideways against his encircling arm.

"Of course," he continued thoughtfully, "if you really want points . . ."

Opening one eye, she caught the twitch at the corners of his mouth. *If you can't fight 'em, join 'em.* "I'm not fussy, but what about authenticity? How did those old warriors cope with iron points digging into them?"

"Ah, well, I'd imagine that when the pampering heated up, the Valkyries took the damn things off."

"That's one possibility. Or maybe that's why the warriors wore those wolfskins. Sort of padding against the wounds of love."

Dag groaned and shook his head at her. "No one told me you did puns. Hmmm. Wolfskins may have been all right in Norseland, but they'd be rather stifling around here, even in the winter. Remember, this pampering is going on indoors, and with central heat..."

Shay lifted her head and shook a finger under his nose, chiding, "Conserve energy; wear your wolfskins to bed."

Dag wiggled his eyebrows *á la* Groucho Marx, gave her a grin that was positively X-rated, and purred, "Save a wolf; take your Valkyrie to bed."

"You're impossible," Shay moaned, dropping her head to let her forehead rest on his shoulder.

"You'll manage just fine." His warm breath feathered over her ear. "I'm having second thoughts about these breastplates. Let's not bother with them at all." His voice dropped to a sensual murmur. "You don't really need them, you know. Your breasts are lovely and firm without any help, and besides, I much prefer warm, soft flesh in my hands."

"Oh, you beast," she muttered, tightening her abdominal muscles against the hot, hollowing arousal deep in her body. Her breasts felt achingly full, and she was appalled at the strength of her need to feel his hands on her. She had completely forgotten where they were until a burst of male laughter shocked her fuzzy mind back to alertness.

"Coffee," she gasped in a strangled voice, hurriedly swinging away from him and becoming very busy straightening her socks. A quick look around was somewhat reassuring. Most of the men had left for other parts of the building, and the few who remained were playing cards and chess on the far side of the room.

By the time Dag returned with coffee and a couple of sandwiches, Shay was quite properly seated on her half of the settee.

"Chicken salad okay?" he asked, dropping down beside her and depositing his loot on the small table.

"Fine. Where did you find the sandwiches?"

"There's a huge stack of them by the coffee urn. Did you hear the radio report?"

Shay glanced at the clock and was stunned to see that it was almost nine. She'd been so distracted by Dag's Valkyrie nonsense that she'd forgotten all about the hurricane. *Maybe*

*that should be Shay the Mush-Minded! Damn, I will not let
him do this to me.*

"I couldn't hear it from here. What's happening?"

"It's come on land farther west than they expected. The
eye will pass almost over Providence, Rhode Island. The
islands and the Cape are getting badly battered. Commu-
nications are patchy, and they're not getting much hard
information yet, but there have been some deaths."

"What about us?"

"It's apparently slowed down over the land, but we're
starting to feel the leading edge now."

Shay automatically looked toward the windows, but between the blackness outside and the wide strips of tape across
the glass, it was impossible to see anything but the sheets
of rain hitting the wide panes. She stared at the half-eaten
sandwich in her hand as a frisson of dread spread through
her body.

"Shay." Dag's voice penetrated her abstracted state, and
she looked at him inquiringly. "They'll be all right, love.
Phyllis has been through this before, and King and Kong
are really quite capable. There's more to them than muscle."

"How did you know—" Shay stopped and stared at him,
her brows drawing together in a scowl. "I do wish you'd
quit reading my mind," she complained.

"I'm not really. Didn't you know that you have a very
expressive face? And I'm beginning to know you rather
well, so I can often guess what's going through your head."
He grinned at her ruefully. "After all, I need all the advantages I can get with you. You're a very stubborn lady.
Almost any other woman would leap at the chance to be a
Valkyrie."

"For you?"

"Uh uh. Mine has to be really special. So far, you're the
first possibility I've found in thirty-six years." He caught
her gaze and held it as he promised, "I don't intend to let
you get away, sweetheart."

Shay watched him consideringly as she finished her sandwich. Finally she sat back and propped her feet on the low
table. There was a strong tinge of regret in her voice as she
said, "I really think you're shooting for the wrong basket

this time. I'm not the handmaiden type, you know. It's truly not in me to cater to a man, to be at his beck and call, to drop everything and come at a whistle."

Leaning back beside her and keeping his eyes fixed on the coffee cup in his hand, Dag said slowly, "That must have been some guy you were married to. As I recall from what you said last night, he also expected you to hand over any money you made, to say nothing of coping on your own for months at a time, never knowing where he was or when he might be back. I can't believe you took all that without complaining."

"Complaining is a very mild term for what I did. I'd say, conservatively, that I threw the longest running temper tantrum in history. The last time I saw him, which was about a year and a half after he'd taken off and left me flat broke, he'd followed me to this little restaurant near where I worked and invited himself to have lunch with me. I couldn't believe it. There he sat—butter wouldn't melt in his lying mouth—and demanded that I hand over five hundred dollars! He didn't ask, mind you, he demanded. I said nothing doing, and he started to get nasty. Everyone was beginning to stare, and I just wanted to get out of there. Cary lost his temper, jumped up, and started calling me every rotten name he could think of. That was it. I just let 'er rip, stood up, and belted him one."

"And?"

"He swung back, I saw red, and the next thing I knew he was sitting on the sidewalk with the strangest look on his face and pieces of plate glass all around him."

"You threw him through the window?" Dag asked in an awed tone.

"Ah . . . not exactly. It . . . well, it was more like a judo thing. I'd picked up a bit here and there."

"What did he do then?"

"Nothing. The people in the restaurant all started clapping, and Angelo, the owner, came charging over and shook his fist at Cary, yelling 'Look what you did to my window, you hoodlum. Get out of here before I call the cops.' I guess it was pretty funny. At least, everyone started laughing, and Angelo pushed me into a chair and insisted on buying me another lunch. Cary took off, and I paid for the window."

Dag was very quiet for a few minutes. Shay finished her coffee and leaned back to rest her head against the wall. She could hear a muted roaring sound and realized it must be the wind. Listening to it, she tried to blank her mind to what was happening outside. There was absolutely nothing she could do right now to help anyone. And Dag was right—there was no need to worry about Phyllis and the boys. They were as safe as she was.

"Shay? Are you going to sleep?"

"In the middle of a hurricane? Don't be silly. I'm just listening to the wind."

"Hmmm. Shay, why do—What's all that?"

There was a commotion in the hallway outside—men's voices calling, a woman crying—then the door opened and a trooper led two young women into the room. The girls, who looked about nineteen or twenty, were white-faced and trembling, and the taller of them was sobbing. Wet hair straggled down their backs, the hems of their jeans were dripping, and their tennis shoes squelched as they walked over to a table and collapsed into a couple of chairs.

Shay recognized Jim Dysart as the trooper who had come in with them, and she waited until he had finished giving quiet instructions to a couple of the men before quietly speaking his name.

"Dysart?"

He came across the room, swung a chair around, and straddled it. "They must have a guardian angel on overtime," he said, shaking his head wonderingly. "They were in a safe place, but got worrying that they'd left a window open in their dorm. So, over everyone's protests, they jumped in their trusty little Datsun and headed for the campus. Did they get the message when they had to turn back on two streets because of downed trees? Oh, no. They decided to try the long way around. Didn't it bother them just a bit that they were getting pushed all over the road by the wind? 'Course not. After all, everyone knows how the news media exaggerate things to make a good story."

"Ah, youth," sighed Shay, grinning at Dysart's disgusted expression. "Wasn't it lovely when we knew all the answers?"

"Yeah." Reluctantly, he mustered an answering grin, and

then finally a laugh. "But I'd like to believe I was never that stupid."

"What changed their minds?" Dag asked.

"Their dandy Datsun got blown off the road—fortunately into a boxwood hedge that kept it from flipping. Also, fortunately, it was two doors from here, and one of the guys out front happened to be looking out the window and saw the headlights waving around. A couple of the men went out and brought them in."

Shay looked over to where the two girls were sitting, now wrapped in blankets and drinking coffee. Three of the younger troopers were sitting at the table talking with them, and Shay noticed that the color had come back to the girls' faces and the shocked look had disappeared. In fact, they seemed to be quite enjoying themselves.

"There's going to be a lot of that," Shay said resignedly. Catching the questioning looks on Dysart's and Dag's faces, she explained, "Small cars blown around. This is one of the strongest hurricanes we've ever had, and in the past they've blown full-size cars and even some trucks over. This time, with so many more small cars, we're going to have a lot more to untangle."

Dysart nodded in agreement. "Can you imagine what some of the car dealers' lots are going to look like? Even worse, there are sure to be more damn fools like those two who simply refuse to believe the warnings." He stood up and stretched. "It's going to be a long, rotten night and an even longer, tougher day tomorrow. See you two later."

Shay and Dag leaned back, putting their feet back up on the coffee table and resting their heads against the wall. For a while, neither said anything. The Barracks had its own power source, but to conserve fuel half the lights had been turned off, and the corner where Shay and Dag were sitting was pleasantly dim. The storm was steadily intensifying, and the voices across the room were lost in the roar of the wind around the building and the smashing of rain against the windows. Occasionally they heard thumps and scrapes as wind-borne debris was flung against the building.

"You look tired."

Shay opened her eyes and turned her head to find him watching her with a look of concern on his face. "Guess I am . . . a little." She noted the fatigue lines around his eyes and a tenseness to his jaw. "You're not exactly leaping with energy yourself. You worked a lot harder than I did to-day . . . thanks to this habit you've developed of yelling at me every time I pick up anything heavier than a toolbox."

"Mmmm . . . meant to speak to you about that toolbox," he said, a gleam of laughter brightening his eyes.

"Never mind," she said, chuckling. "I refuse to get into another argument with you until the bruises from the last one fade."

Dag looked far from repentant as he arched an eyebrow and drawled, "Ah, now, if you'd like to compare bruises, I've got a beauty on my shin."

"Well, if anyone should ask you for your fingerprints, send them to me—I've got a full set on my arms."

"You came within an ace of having a matching palm print on your butt," he said provocatively.

Shay studied the challenging sparkle in his dark eyes, debated briefly with herself, and then surprised both of them by quickly leaning toward him and kissing him on the nose. "Fry ice," she said blandly and settled back on her half of the couch.

"We'll save it for later," he promised, "when you're back in fighting trim. Lift your head."

"Why?" But she was tilting her head forward as she said it.

His answer was to slide his arm around her and ease her over so her head rested in the hollow of his shoulder. He turned slightly so that his lips brushed her forehead as he murmured, "Better?"

"Mmmmm." Shay knew this was a mistake. She should move away from him, and she would—soon. But for just a few minutes, it was so comfortable to be held. And so warm, especially where the whole length of her leg was pressed against his. Surely five minutes couldn't hurt any-thing. Or even ten minutes—just to rest her eyes a while . . . and his shoulder really was . . .

chapter 7

IT WAS THE pain in her ear that dragged her out of sleep. Blinking her heavy eyelids and trying to keep them open, her mind fuzzy and disoriented, Shay murmured protestingly at the sharp pain and tried to fling her hand up to brush away whatever was causing it. She couldn't move her hands.

"Shay. Come on, sweetheart, wake up. It's almost time to go. Shay."

The insistent voice at her ear, coupled with warm lips nuzzling her earlobe as a moist tongue soothed the pain away, finally brought her eyes wide open and cleared the fog from her brain.

"Dag, what the hell are you doing?" Her voice was hoarse from sleep. "Did you *bite* me? Why are you holding my hands? Let go."

"You sleep like you've been clubbed over the head." He removed the restraining hold he'd had on her hands and pulled her upright to sit beside him. "And I was holding your hands so you wouldn't belt me. It's taken me five minutes to wake you up," he said plaintively. "Biting your ear was my next to last resort."

Yawning and rubbing her eyes, she mumbled, "What was your last resort?"

"Kissing you, but you know where that leads us. I didn't think you'd appreciate waking up and finding yourself the center of attention."

For the first time, Shay looked around the room and discovered that it was full of people, most of whom seemed to be eating or drinking. "What's happening?"

Dag stood and stretched, then reached down to pull her to her feet. "We've got about half an hour to get ready to go. Come on. I'll point you toward the ladies' room, and then we'll get something to eat."

Shay looked at him in bewilderment. "Time to go? But the hur—" Her gaze focused across his shoulder at the clock on the wall. "Quarter past two! You mean I slept through the whole thing?" she squealed incredulously.

"You won't believe what you slept through. Look over there." Dag turned her to the right and waved his hand at the windows.

"Good grief!" she yelped, staring at the remains of a huge tree limb that had obviously blown through one of the windows and was firmly jammed in the frame, held there by the mass of small branches and leaves. The limb projected some three feet into the room, ending in a smooth, squared-off surface.

"You not only snoozed through the crash, but you never so much as twitched when one of the men used a power saw to cut the rest of it off. And if you didn't hear any of that, you certainly didn't hear the two cars that were smashed against the building, or the four other windows that were blown in."

Shay shook her head ruefully and moaned, "I'll never hear the end of this."

"You know it," agreed Dag, laughing. He caught her hand and started for the door. "Let's get cleaned up and eat."

On her way across the room, Shay fielded a number of teasing comments with some laughing quips of her own, and by the time she and Dag returned and sat down to eat, the men were deep in speculation on what they would find outside. It was two-forty when they all gathered in the ready room to get assignments and instructions. By three o'clock, Shay and Dag had donned their boots and rain gear, collected emergency equipment, and were waiting by the back exit for Dysart and Brady.

The two big troopers, both in their thirties, each with

over ten years on the force, strode down the hallway followed by two young rookies. All of them were carrying powerful, battery-pack lights, and Dysart and one of the rookies were shouldering large cartons packed with pressure splints, trauma blankets, and bandages. They added their gear to the pile beside Shay and Dag. Brady handed Shay a powerful, police-type walkie-talkie, pulled a clipboard from under his arm, and started checking off a list, giving a running commentary as he went along.

"Keep that with you so we don't lose touch. Hope this inspires you to get a CB, Shay. You understand how we're working this, don't you? Jim and I will each drive a cruiser, Bill Reardon will ride with Jim, and Stan Carlson will be with me. Shay, you stick with us; our three vehicles will work as a team. Remember, we don't care about wrecked cars right now unless they've got people in them or they're blocking a clear passage on the road. We don't have to clear the whole road at this point, just enough room to get emergency vehicles through. Our main aim is to locate anyone injured or trapped. You've only got four power saws here, Shay."

"Mine's in the truck."

"Oxygen cylinders? Spare gas? How do you want to handle those?"

"I'll carry the gas cans," said Shay. "They'll be safer. I've got clamps to hold them in place. You two take the oxygen. We aren't going to be that far apart."

"Fine. What about the medical supplies? I know you carry a pretty complete kit on the truck. Do you need any of this?"

"I restocked my locker before I left, but I'd better take a few extra splints and blankets. These two kits are for you, to supplement the ones you already have in the cars."

"Okay. Guess we're ready," Brady announced. "At least we don't have to worry about getting zapped by the downed power lines; everything in this area's been shut off."

"That may be the only blessing we have," Shay muttered pessimistically.

"What the hell is that? Can you make it out, Dag?"

"Looks like the whole road is blocked. Better stop here

and let me go ahead with a light. All that glitter must be glass."

"Go on, then. I'll call the others."

A blast of rain sprayed across the cab as Dag pushed open the door and got out, carrying one of the big battery-pack lanterns. Shay watched him move out in front of the truck, the orange flashers gleaming intermittently across his jacket. They were in the tail end of the hurricane, although the wind had decreased to between seventy and eighty miles an hour. It was still raining heavily, and small pieces of debris continued to fly through the air.

Shay glanced at Dag's watch, which was hanging from the rearview mirror, and grimaced. It had taken them over an hour to cover less than two miles of their sector of Route 9. Not that she was complaining. On the contrary, she was feeling a bit more optimistic now. So far, they hadn't found anyone with serious injuries—nothing more than minor cuts and bruises. Of course, they hadn't made a building-by-building search yet, but both the cruisers and the truck had been moving very slowly and had their flashers on. While the three drivers concentrated on the road, the others had been keeping as close a watch as possible in the stormy darkness for signs of anyone signaling to them.

Peering through the rain-smeared windshield, Shay strained to see what Dag was doing. She could barely make out his big form moving off to the left, almost out of range of the headlights. Although she could just see the glow of the light he was carrying as it swept across the dark wall of rain, she couldn't make out the details of what was in front of him. She squinted at the side mirror to locate the cruisers she'd left some hundred yards back. Brady and Dysart had decided to check out a couple of restaurants and a motel, while she and Dag continued clearing the road. So far, they'd had little difficulty, although it had taken some time to push several cars to one side, sweep up broken glass, and drag several large tree limbs out of the two lanes they were clearing.

Shay spotted one set of blue and red flashers moving up behind her, and then saw the other set some way back and to the left. The walkie-talkies crackled with static, and then Dysart's voice came in, breaking up slightly with the interference but still understandable as he reported that several people in the motel had been cut by flying glass and that he and Reardon would be there for a few minutes to administer first aid.

Brady acknowledged Dysart and then called Shay, asking why she was stopped.

"There's what looks like a ton of glass all over the road, and beyond that something massive all the way across. Dag's gone ahead with a light to see what it is."

"I can't see him," Brady said, "Where is he?"

"Somewhere over to the left. I can't—No, wait, there he is, coming back this way but from the right."

Sensing something radically wrong from the way Dag was moving, Shay pushed open the door and slid out. Glass crunched under her boots as she struggled to close the door, and she welcomed the slicker-clad arm that came over her shoulder to help.

"Thanks, Brady," she said, turning around and catching at his arm to keep her balance against the wind. "I think we've got trouble."

Carlson joined them, and the three crunched their way to the front of the truck to meet Dag.

"What is it?" asked Shay, raising her voice to be heard over the storm noise.

"A mess," Dag answered succinctly as the four of them gathered in the glare of the headlights. Shay could see that his face looked pale and his mouth was tight with tension. "There's a big tractor-trailer rig on its side, and ten or so cars from that foreign car dealer's lot over there have blown across the road and piled up against the rig like driftwood. They're all every which way, and I didn't dare try to climb over them, but I think there's a van half under the truck cab."

There was something in his voice that sent a chill racing through Shay, and she caught his hand tightly, saying urgently, "Dag?"

"I could hear someone calling. I'm sure there're people in the van, and I think I saw something in the truck cab."

"Carlson, call Dysart and tell him to get over here as soon as he can," said Brady. "Dag, where exactly are the van and the cab?"

Dag turned and pointed, speaking quickly. "In the middle of these two lanes, but on the far side of the cars. We can't get around to the right; it's blocked with a collapsed building. We may be able to get through on the left. The light standards along the dealer's lot are down, but I think we can crawl through."

"Let's do it," said Brady. "We need a couple more lights and a medical kit." He started back toward the cruiser at a lurching run.

"There's glass everywhere," Dag said as he and Shay headed for the back of the truck. "Better put some gloves on to protect your hands."

The winds of the hurricane had turned the tall aluminum light poles lining the car lot into a bent and twisted obstacle course, dotted here and there with crumpled cars that looked, in the spooky, rain-washed darkness, like so many flies caught in an erratic web woven by a drunken spider. It took the four of them almost ten minutes to work their careful way through the mess.

"Shay!" yelled Dag from somewhere ahead of her, and Shay blinked as a light steadied on her face and then lowered to shine on the ground in front of her. "Take my hand. I'm clear now."

Guided the last few feet by the strong grip of his hand, Shay finally straightened up and got a good look at the massive tangle of dented, torn, and mangled vehicles.

The three men spread out, directing the bright beams of their lanterns over the truck cab and the brightly painted van jammed beneath it. Shay could hear Brady talking to Dysart on the walkie-talkie he carried, but she couldn't make out what he was saying. Shifting the heavy first-aid box to her other hand, she flexed her cramped fingers and then raised her hand to block the rain from her eyes. She kept shifting her gaze from the treacherous footing to the bulk of the cab and van.

Dag, a few feet in front of her, and Carlson, who was working his way around to the left, started calling, then pausing and calling again. Shay thought she heard an answering shout, and concentrated on kicking a path through the debris, quickly moving up beside Dag.

"Where's it coming from, the van or the truck?"

"The van, I think," Dag answered, swinging his light to the right. "It's easier going this way, around this mess." The light came back to indicate the flattened remains of a small sports car blocking their direct path to the van.

"Brady! Can you hear me?" yelled Carlson.

They could see his light signaling from the front of the van, which was on its side and half-crushed under the big truck cab tilted against it.

"Yo!" Brady bellowed.

"Five people in van," Carlson called. "One dead, two in bad shape. Driver's still in truck. Can't get at them."

Shay, Dag, and Brady were now at the rear of the van and could hear the hysterical cries of a girl and the deeper, gasping tones of a man talking to Carlson. Kicking a space clear, Shay set the medical kit down on the pavement and moved up beside Dag. She could now hear moans of pain from the van, but she tried to block out the sound, knowing she had to concentrate first on figuring out a way to open up the van.

"Let me have the light for a minute, Dag."

Using both hands, she swung the big lantern up to shoulder height and started playing it slowly along the side of the van—now the top—and the looming truck cab. Dag put a supporting hand under the heavy light while Brady moved up beside them and added the power of his lantern on a parallel path.

"Hold it, Brady," Shay said as their lights hit the cab window. "Too much glare. Move over a couple of feet. There. Can you see him?"

The cab was leaning at an almost forty-five-degree angle, but they could make out the motionless head and shoulder of a man slumped against the window.

"Any way to get that door open, Shay?" Brady asked.

"Uh uh. It's jammed at the bottom against the van." Shay shifted the beam of her light to the back of the cab and the twisted linkage between cab and trailer. She turned back to Brady and Dag.

"We need to get the wrecker around here. There's no way into the van except to rip it open. But we can't do that until we get the cab off it. Once we remove any of the vertical parts of the van, we weaken it, and it may not hold up that cab. Brady, what's the chances of getting another heavy-duty wrecker out here for half an hour or so? We really need it."

"Thought we might. Dysart's already called for one. He and Reardon have been clearing a path through that glass, and they're backing your truck around to the narrowest point of that mess." Brady waved a hand at the tumble of cars across the road. "I think there's one place where, if we haul out two, maybe three, cars, we can open up enough space to get the truck through."

"Okay," Shay agreed, her eyes fixed on the tractor cab above her. She turned back to Brady and asked, "How about letting Dysart and Reardon do that? Jim's given me a hand often enough that he knows how to handle the hoisting rig. While they're doing that, I want to see if we can get the driver out of that cab before we try to pull it off the van."

"Shay . . ."

"Let's see how bad things are in the van first."

Shay reached for the medical kit, but Dag's hand on her shoulder held her back, and he picked up the kit and started for the front of the van. They found Carlson crouched on his knees close to the distorted remains of the front end, carefully removing the rest of the shattered windshield, piece by piece. In the bright beam of the lantern, which Carlson had positioned to shine into the van, they could see the bodies of two young men held in the twisted frames of the front seats and, behind them, the slow movements of another man and a girl.

As the other three crouched around him, Carlson broke off the monologue of reassurance that he was directing at the couple in the van and reported tersely, "College students. Thought it would be a kick to take a ride in the hurricane and see the action. Watch the glass, Shay." He shifted to one side as Shay reached through a large hole to press her fingers against the neck of the limp figure jammed behind the steering wheel.

"I got a pulse on him a few minutes ago," continued Carlson. "Couldn't get even a flutter on the other one. Bob, the guy in the back, says there's another girl who's unconscious. He thinks she's got a broken leg and maybe a broken shoulder. The other girl has a broken arm and some cuts.

He's sure he's got cracked ribs, and his leg's broken in at least two places. Also has cuts; they all do."

"Does he know how long they've been here?" asked Shay, who was now, along with Dag and Brady, working on removing the rest of the windshield.

"They went out about ten, right when it was hitting high gear. Played dodg'em with falling trees on the side streets, then decided to come out to the highway to see if Gill's was open." Carlson's tone was one of angry disgust. "They'd gone through most of a case of beer and decided to top their party off with a pizza." Shay didn't quite catch his grunted three-word description of the unbelievably stupid students.

Pulling off her right glove again, Shay leaned over to speak into Dag's ear. "Can you brace your arm across here for me to lean against? I think I can reach this other one with the stethoscope. Brady!" she called. "Hand me the stethoscope from the kit."

It only took a couple of minutes for Shay to be sure that the young man in the passenger seat was beyond help. The driver was still alive but in very poor condition.

"His legs are pinned, maybe crushed, and I'm sure he's got internal injuries." Shay was tight-lipped, but she spoke in a calm, even voice. "Until we can get this thing open, there's not much we can do for any of them."

She stood up and moved a few feet away from the van, followed by Dag and Brady. When Carlson started to stand, she put a restraining hand on his shoulder. "Why don't you stay there and keep talking to them? That girl's on the edge of hysteria, and if she starts flinging herself around in there, she could hurt the others as well as do more damage to herself." Stepping closer to Dag and Brady, she said, "Let's see if we can get that truck driver out, if he's still alive. I think I can—"

"Shay—" Brady tried in interrupt.

"Listen," she said forcefully, "I'm no feather, but I'm still much lighter than either of you. We shouldn't put any more weight on that cab than we have to, especially if whoever goes up there has to move around much. Now come on. I think I can get up there easily, without jarring anything, by climbing up over the linkage."

Shay bent over the medical kit, selected a few items,

and stuffed them into her jacket pocket along with the stethoscope. As she and the two men hurried back to the rear of the cab, they could hear the scraping and crashing of metal from where Dysart and Reardon were clearing an opening in the pile-up of cars.

"Shay, take the walkie-talkie," Brady said, catching up to her and pushing it into her hand. "Tony just got a message from one of the McCormick boys."

"Go ahead, Tony."

"Art McCormick just called on the CB. He's been over to your place. Everyone's fine." Shay pressed the receiver closer to her ear, trying to hear through the static. "Can you hear me, Shay? Everyone's okay at your house."

"Got it, Tony."

"You lost some trees, a few windows, and part of the front veranda."

"Who cares, as long as I didn't lose a kid or Phyllis!" said Shay, laughing shakily with relief. "Thanks, Tony. Thank the McCormicks if they call again."

"Right. Let me talk to Brady."

Shay handed the radio back to Brady and moved up beside Dag. He'd placed one of the lanterns on top of the van so that it would shine on the cab window, and was now waiting beside the misshapen linkage between the cab and trailer, holding the other lantern.

"Did you hear?" asked Shay. At his negative headshake, she repeated Tony's message.

His grin flashed as he chided, "Told you not to worry, King and Kong would take care of them. You ready to tackle this now?"

"Let's go."

With Dag's firm hands on her hips helping her to keep her balance against the diminishing but still-strong wind, Shay climbed up on the linkage. As she reached the angled slope of the cab, she felt his hands slide away, the right one lingering just long enough to deliver an encouraging pat on her bottom. Carefully, she worked her way along until she could reach the door handle, while Dag and Brady scrambled over the linkage to stand ready below her in case she slipped on the wet, leaf-splattered metal.

"Shay," called Brady, "we can reach the bottom edge of

the door. If you can get it open far enough against the wind, we'll help you ease it over."

She waved an acknowledging hand, saving her breath for the struggle with the door. Muttering curses, she tried to find a position to give herself leverage. The wind was pinning her flat against the side of the cab while she fought to open the door the few inches necessary for Brady and Dag to get a firm grip on it. Finally they managed it, and Shay eased her long legs into the cab and slowly, alert to any shift in the cab's position, braced her feet and slid down along the seat until she could reach the unconscious driver.

Moving swiftly but carefully, she examined him.

"Is he alive?" called Brady.

"Yes," Shay yelled back. "Can't find anything broken. I think he's concussed. Got a lump on his head. I'm going to see if I can bring him around. It'll be easier to get him out of here if he's not dead weight. He's too big for me to drag up to the door."

It took Shay another ten minutes or so to bring the driver around, and even then he was groggy and only vaguely aware of what was happening.

"Don't move yet. Tell me your name. What's your name?"

Shay's voice was insistent but calm, and finally the man mumbled, "Crawley."

"Okay, Crawley, now open your eyes and look at me. That's it. I'm Shay, and I'm going to help you out of here."

"'S wrong?"

"You had an accident in the storm. The cab's tilted. See it?"

"Yeah. Shay?"

"That's right, Shay. Now we have to move very carefully up to the door. There are two *very* big men out there who will help you down to the ground."

"Head . . . head . . ."

"I'm sure it hurts like hell. You gave it quite a bang. As soon as we get you out of here, you can lie down."

Urging, guiding, and half dragging the large man, Shay finally got him up to the door where Dag and Brady could get hold of him and lift him down to the ground. Shay leaned, panting, against the door frame, her arms trembling from the strain of hauling Crawley's heavy, semi-conscious body up the sloping seat. She watched Dag straighten and turn back to her.

"You all right?" he asked.

"Yeah. Just getting my breath back. He's heavy, and he couldn't help much."

Dag reached up and grasped her dangling legs behind the knees. "Brace your feet against my shoulders and slide down to sit on the running board. I'll lift you off."

In seconds, he was swinging her easily to the ground. Even though she had felt his bulging shoulder muscles under her hands, she was still surprised at the ease with which he handled her hundred-forty or so pounds. She didn't have time to dwell on the unexpectedly pleasant feeling. With a sure instinct, Dag had deduced her physical state and was busy rubbing life back into her numb biceps.

"Stand still for a minute, sweetheart. Brady's taking the driver around to the other side. Dysart and Reardon have brought the truck and both cruisers through, and there are a couple of ambulances on the way. Feel better?"

"Fine."

"Come on, then, we'd better get those kids out of the van."

With a strong arm around her, Dag started walking toward the front of the cab. He paused just before they stepped into the view of the others and tipped her face up to his.

"I wish you didn't have to be in the middle of this. It's—"

Driven by an age-old instinct, Shay turned into his embrace, wrapping her arms tightly around his waist and pressing her face into his neck. It didn't matter that her cheek was against wet plastic or that they were padded with layers of heavy clothing. The strength was there in his arms and in the solid feel of his big body against hers, and that was what she needed at that moment.

"It's not going to be pleasant or easy," she finally said, dread clear in her voice. "But it's something I'm trained for, and they need help. I'll be okay. Really I will. You—"

"I'll be right there with you. Just tell me what you want me to do."

He gave her a quick, reassuring squeeze, and then they

were moving past the cab and into the bright illumination of the cruisers' headlights, which were directed toward the van. With five strong men and a heavy-duty hoist, it was only a matter of minutes before the truck cab was lifted off, the side of the van forced open, and Shay could wriggle in past the twisted frames of the back seats. There was very little room in the van, and Shay had to contort her five feet eleven inches into a series of uncomfortable and cramped positions. While Brady, Carlson, Dysart, and Reardon worked to remove more of the side panels, Dag perched on the edge of the opening with the medical supplies and a radio, handing Shay what she needed and relaying her reports to the hospital emergency room and their instructions back to her.

With practiced expertise Shay blocked out all thoughts and feelings and concentrated solely on immobilizing broken bones, stopping bleeding, checking vital signs, and administering the treatment ordered by the emergency room personnel. She was only vaguely aware of the activities of the men, and the ambulances were almost upon them before she heard the sirens. Reardon's hand on her shoulder and the sound of his voice in her ear startled her into banging her head, since she hadn't heard him approach. She bit off a pithy comment as she realized that they had opened up the whole side of the van, and they could now start removing the injured.

With swift, deft movements, the ambulance attendants and the troopers removed the three people from the back of the van. Shay, much to her relief, could turn over the responsibility for the badly injured driver to the doctor who had come along with the ambulances. Within minutes another tow truck arrived, and Shay was more than happy to return with Dag to her own truck and resume clearing the mass of wreckage from the road.

chapter 8

SHORTLY BEFORE EIGHT-THIRTY Tuesday morning, Shay and Dag, along with Brady and Carlson, were taking a break while Dysart and Reardon took the tow truck and one of the cruisers back to the Barracks to fill the gas tanks. Sitting on a fallen tree trunk at the edge of a motel parking lot near the intersection of Routes 9 and 202, they allowed themselves to relax for the first time in over five hours. They were all tired and disheveled but somewhat cleaner than they'd been before the motel manager provided them with a stack of towels and the use of a lavatory. Few words were spoken among the four of them as they concentrated on the containers of hot, thick beef stew and the ham and cheese sandwiches that had just been delivered by a Red Cross canteen truck.

A guest at the motel had lent them a portable radio, and now, for the first time since the storm ended, they were hearing reports of the full extent of the disaster. In the past few hours they had deliberately not turned on any of their own radios. It had been quite bad enough coping with the dead and injured in their sector, and, as the cold, sad night hours gave way to dawn and they got their first clear look at the terrible devastation left in the wake of the killer storm, they wanted even less to hear any more bad news. It was enough that they knew there were many casualties and widespread damage; they hadn't been ready to hear the details. Now, however, the initial shock had been blunted, and they had had time to come to terms with the scope of the destruction, both human and material. It was time to find out just how much havoc the storm had wreaked.

As the WBZ Storm Center announcer's voice described scenes of devastation and death, Shay unthinkingly hitched a few inches closer to Dag until their shoulders were touching.

He shifted his leg to press against hers, waiting until her eyes focused on him to murmur softly, "Eat that while it's hot, Shay. You need it."

She stared at him with troubled eyes. His face was drawn and pale under the deep tan, his lean cheeks and strong jawline shadowed with an incipient beard. *I wonder why his beard is darker than his hair. I wonder if the hair on his body is dark or light.* Chiding herself for having such a frivolous thought in the midst of so much disastrous news, Shay frowned as she met the concerned look in his dark eyes. Her frown smoothed out, and his expression changed to one of warm reassurance as they again held one of those silent exchanges. After a moment, Shay nodded agreement and slowly resumed eating and listening to the radio reports from the Boston station.

The hurricane had blasted through southern New England on a curving path, leaving a hundred-mile-wide swath of devastation in its wake. The radio announcer's voice broke as he listed the estimated numbers of missing people and described the search efforts.

All of Rhode Island and large portions of Connecticut, Massachusetts, New Hampshire, and Maine had been declared federal disaster areas, and help was on the way from as far away as Ohio and Kentucky. Red Cross disaster teams had started moving in as soon as the worst of the wind died down. Although the governors of the five states had declared states of emergency and closed all roads to any but official and emergency vehicles, there was always the threat of looting in a disaster situation of this magnitude, and National Guard units were being dispersed throughout the area, particularly in the cities and large towns, to guard against looters.

"It's almost like being in the middle of a war," said Brady, reaching to turn down the radio.

"We look like we've been in a war," Shay responded with a wry grimace.

They had all shed their rain gear shortly before dawn, and as the early morning temperatures started to rise to comfortable levels, Shay and Dag had discarded their heavy sweaters and eventually pushed up the sleeves of the cotton-knit pullovers. After hours of administering first aid, often to people cut by flying glass, scrambling over and crawling into wrecked vehicles, clearing away trees, picking their way through rubble to reach the injured, and falling into mud puddles, all four of them really did look as though they'd been on a battlefield. They were spattered with grease, oil, mud, sawdust, blood, and plaster dust. Everything they had on had at least one rip or snag. All of them had received a variety of minor cuts and scrapes, and Carlson sported an elastic bandage on his left wrist.

Shay swung her heavy braid, which was now looking rather frayed, over her shoulder and started picking bits of bark and twigs out of it, as she muttered, "I'd trade my favorite wrench for a brush right now. And some clean clothes."

"Make that some lighter clean clothes," said Dag. "Now that it's warming up, these longjohns and lined jeans are getting a bit uncomfortable."

Brady stood and stretched, groaning at the twinges in his aching muscles. "I'd pass up the clothes for a few hours' sleep. However, I don't think any of us are going to get our wishes for a—"

He broke off as a big Honda motorcycle roared into the parking lot and swept around to stop in front of them. The driver and his passenger were unidentifiable behind the faceplates of their black and gold helmets, but both were wearing armbands designating them as Civil Defense personnel. Before Brady could ask his first question, the passenger scrambled off the bike, pulling off his helmet to disclose a head of bright red curls. Yelling "Mom!" he ran to throw his arms around Shay, nearly knocking her off her feet.

"Marcus! What are you doing here?" Shay hugged him

hard for a long moment, then held him off to look at him anxiously. "Is anything wrong? Is Kyle all right? Is Nana—"

"Nothing's wrong, Mom. Honest." Marcus was looking his mother over from head to foot, and his happy grin faded as he took in her stained and torn appearance. "Wow, are you a mess!" he exclaimed with all the tact of a thirteen-year-old boy. "Is that blood? Are you hurt? What happened?"

"It's not hers," said Dag, placing a calming hand on the boy's shoulder. "Your mother's fine, except for being tired and grubby."

"Thanks a lot," Shay growled, giving him a quick up-and-down look and raising a mocking eyebrow. "You're not exactly a shining vision of the tailor's art, either."

Tossing his hands in the air, Marcus turned with a grin toward the interested troopers and the husky young man who had been driving the motorcycle. "They've been carrying on like this ever since they met. You should have seen the fight they had yesterday. Dag—"

"Marcus!" yelled Shay. "That's enough. Hi, Art," she said as she caught sight of the bike's owner. "How did you let Marcus talk you into this?"

"He didn't," answered Art McCormick, laughing. "It was your mother. She said you'd be wanting some cooler clothes and some food, and she asked Dad if one of us could get through on the bike and try to find you. All the roads out of the village are blocked with fallen trees and telephone poles, and some of them are flooded. The only way out is to go cross country. Marcus insisted on coming to make sure you were okay, even though Sergeant Clinton had sent messages that you were fine."

"How'd you find us?" Shay asked.

"Called the Barracks on the CB," Art said, waving a hand at the radio on the elaborate control panel inside the bike's wraparound windscreen. He ambled over to the bike, opened the big saddlebags mounted on either side of the rear wheel, and started pulling out canvas tote bags and large Thermos bottles. "Your mother said one Thermos was soup and the other two are coffee. One of these bags . . . this one . . . is packed full of sandwiches and plastic bowls of salad stuff, and I saw her put in a couple of cucumbers and some apples. The other bags have clean clothes, and she said to tell you to check the side pockets because she put in toothbrushes and paste and your hairbrush."

Shay and Dag lugged everything over to the tree trunk and started investigating the bags of clothing.

"We'll save the food for later. We've just eaten," said Shay, holding up a pair of tan cord jeans that were obviously too long for her. "These must be Dad's. Here, Dag, she's packed stuff for you, too."

"And this bag is definitely meant for you," Dag murmured for her ears alone, handing her the navy blue tote and taking the brown one from her hands. "Maybe I'll rethink my ideas on proper Valkyrie attire."

Shay gave him a questioning look and then, seeing the wicked amusement in his eyes, looked down into the navy tote. "Oh, damn," she muttered as she saw the leopard-print nylon bikini briefs Dag had spread artistically over the top of the folded clothes. *Mother, what I'm going to do to you!*

She was saved from trying to think of a suitable comment by Marcus's timely arrival.

"Hey, Mom, you should see the front piazza. A huge chunk of the maple came down on the roof, and it broke two windows in Nana's room and flattened half the piazza and broke the big window in the den. And you know the big blue spruce beyond the fish pond? It fell down and wiped out half the lilac hedge and cracked the edge of the pond. Oh, yeah, and a big metal trash can blew across the yard from somewhere and smashed one of the windows in the sunroom. Isn't it lucky we taped them all?"

Marcus was in full spate, and Shay and Dag, unable to get a word in edgewise, dropped down onto the tree trunk and gave him their full attention as he excitedly described his cross-country ride with Art. His voice was full of pride and a self-assurance that made Shay bite her lip as he displayed his CD armband and explained how Mr. McCormick had assigned him to assist Art in checking the condition of the country roads and the outlying farms around Beech Village.

Marcus was finally running out of steam when Brady glanced around and waved a signaling arm as Dysart and

Reardon turned into the lot. "Have you got enough gas?" he asked Art. "Shay has several cans on the truck if you need some."

Before Art could answer, Shay said, "Just to be on the safe side, you'd better top off your tank. You probably won't find any between here and home."

"Yeah, I know," Art agreed. "Good thing you gave the station keys to Dad. He's already doled out most of the gas you left in the cans inside for the power saws, and when we left he was rigging up the hand-crank on one of the pumps, like you told him to. Those guys who stayed at your house were going to man it."

"Fine. Tell him to use whatever he needs. There's plenty."

"Okay, Shay. Come on, Marcus, we'd better get going. We've still got a lot of ground to cover."

Shay put an arm around her tall son and started walking with him and Art toward the bike. "You two be careful. Marcus, you know where all the EMT supplies are at the house. Give Mr. McCormick and Mr. Stoner anything they need. Okay? And I don't want you or Kyle climbing on any roofs or into any of the trees. There're a lot of weakened limbs just waiting for a nudge to come crashing down, and you with 'em. Hear me?"

"Don't worry, Mom," said Marcus with exaggerated patience and a teasing grin. "Kyle and a bunch of the kids are helping the men clear the road around the Green, and Mr. McCormick said I could help Art."

Marcus picked up his helmet and then hesitated with it in one hand as he took a quick look around at the waiting men. Finally, with a what-the-heck shrug, he threw his arms around his mother and gave her a quick, hard hug and a restrained kiss on the cheek. Shay, understanding his feelings about "mushy stuff," confined herself to a similar good-bye.

A minute later she came close to giving her elder son a whack on the bottom when he turned to Dag, held out his hand for a man-to-man handshake, and said confidingly, "Keep an eye on her, Dag. She gets into the weirdest messes sometimes. She won't admit there's anything she can't do. Kyle and I have an awful time with her."

Casting a sideways look at his mother's wrathful face,

Marcus prudently removed himself to the far side of the motorcycle. Encouraged by the men's chuckles, he added with a grin, "Remind us to tell you about the time she tried to rescue a kitten from the tower roof, and—"

"Marcus," Shay growled threateningly, "one more word out of you and your brother's going to be an only child."

Laughing, Dag slung an arm around her shoulders and winked at the tall boy. "Be easy, Marcus. I've got her under control."

He grabbed Shay's arm with his free hand just in time to keep her from jabbing him in the ribs with her elbow. With a grin that had her grinding her teeth in frustration, he chided, "Now, now, sweetheart, no violence in front of the kids."

Shay's reply was fortunately drowned out as Art kicked over the starter and revved up the engine. With farewell waves the boys wheeled out of the parking lot and sped out of sight.

"Okay, everybody," said Dysart, calling them back to the business at hand. "We're to continue along Route 9 as far as Ware, then work back, checking out the side roads for people needing medical assistance. Road crews are on the way to start clearing trees, so with luck, Shay, all you'll have to tow will be cars."

"What about all the vehicles we left in the outside lanes on Route 9?" she asked.

"Not our problem," Dysart answered. "We're to concentrate on making a clear passage for emergency vehicles any way we can, as fast as we can. By tonight there'll be Army units as well as Guard units here with heavy-duty towing equipment. They'll take care of whatever we have to leave. If everyone's ready, let's go."

Shay and Dag begged five minutes to change. Feeling almost normal again in clean jeans and tee-shirts, they stowed the tote bags and Thermoses in one of the lockers on the back of the truck.

"Want me to drive for a while?" Dag asked as he secured the locker cover.

"If you don't mind," Shay replied. "I've got to catch up on the log book while I can still remember what we've done. Those notes I made on what we towed and pushed out of the way are practically illegible."

Dag led the way out of the parking lot and turned east on Route 9, holding the truck to the middle of the road and keeping his speed down to twenty miles an hour. He slowed to a near stop at all vehicles along the sides of the road to make sure they were empty.

"It was thoughtful of your mother to send toothbrushes, to say nothing of a razor."

"Hmmm? Oh, yes, wasn't it?" Shay answered distractedly. Then his remark registered, and she glanced over at him. "My word, you did shave, didn't you? She must have dug out Dad's battery-powered shaver."

"I'm surprised it still works."

"It probably didn't," said Shay, chuckling. "What do you want to bet she got Ev to open the store and find her some batteries?"

"Would he—Uh oh, Shay, on the left. Looks like someone's hurt."

While Dag manuevered around two abandoned cars and a parked truck, Shay leaned forward and swore feelingly as her gaze went past the wildly waving man, his head wrapped in a makeshift bandage. Behind him, across a dirt parking lot, was the collapsed tangle of what had been a small "family style" restaurant. Shay could recognize nothing of the attractive, one-story frame building in the pile of jutting timbers and broken walls.

Dag stopped beside the man, the two cruisers pulling up behind the truck, and he and Shay exchanged a long look of strength and support before jumping out to face the latest disaster.

chapter 9

"I GUESS IT could have been worse," said Shay wearily.

"Yeah," Dag sighed. "I really expected we'd find more than four . . . beyond help. Out of fifteen who were in Mr. Marini's restaurant when it fell in, that's . . ." He let the sentence trail off, thinking of the young mother who'd done her best to save her daughters, the elderly man who'd shielded his wife only to have her succumb to exposure, and the well-dressed man in his forties whose wallet contained pictures of his four teenagers and his still-lovely wife.

"I don't really want this," Shay muttered as Dag pushed the plastic cup of hot soup into her hands.

"I know, but drink it anyway. You need it; you're half-way into shock yourself."

They were sitting on the ground, leaning against a fallen tree, at the edge of the woods behind Marini's grape arbor, or what was left of it. After the last ambulance had departed, and while the rescue crews were gathering up their gear, Dag had scooped up the Thermos of soup, which Reardon had left when he took the truck, collected a dazed Shay, and led her to this quiet place out of sight of the wrecked building.

Too tired and heartsick at the moment to argue, Shay sipped at the homemade chicken noodle soup, feeling its welcome heat start to melt the chill deep inside her, a chill that had been spreading ever since she'd looked at the woman in the station wagon crushed by a wall of the restaurant and known that they were too late. She made no protest, either, when Dag's arm came to rest across her shoulders and he moved closer to her. With a sigh, almost of relief, she closed her eyes and let her head rest against his shoulder.

"Why don't you sleep until Reardon gets back?" Dag suggested, taking the tipping cup out of her hand and sipping at it himself.

"Can't," Shay protested in a low, hoarse voice. "If I go to sleep now, you'll never wake me up. I just want to relax and unwind for a bit and try to put all that out of my mind." She waved a limp hand toward the arbor and what was beyond it.

"Okay."

Before Shay could open her heavy eyelids, she felt herself lifted and swung. By the time she was fully alert, she was sitting between Dag's long legs with her back resting against the solid wall of his chest.

His warm lips and equally warm breath feathered across her cheek as he said softly, "Now, I'm going to unwind you, and we're going to talk about something that has nothing at all to do with this or any other hurricane."

"What?" gasped Shay as his very large, very firm hands started kneading the sore muscles in her upper arms, gradually working their way up to her shoulders and taut neck.

"Stretch your legs out and cross your ankles. You'll be more comfortable. Let's see, what shall we discuss? Hmmmm . . . well, for starters, I've been wondering why you go by Shay MacAllister rather than Severin."

"I never felt like a Severin. Maybe the infatuation died too fast, before Cary and I had a chance to build any kind of a foundation as a couple. He went his way, and I was left to my own devices. It was the MacAllister in me that I leaned on and used. Weird. I've never really figured it out before. I just felt like Shay MacAllister, and when we came back here, it seemed natural—with the station and all—to call myself that."

"Don't people ever wonder about your name being different from the boys'?"

"Not in a small New England village, they don't," Shay

responded, chuckling. "Believe me, everybody knows everything about everybody else. It's impossible to keep a secret. On the other hand, no one would dream of asking me why I'm still using my maiden name when I'm a legitimate widow. Eccentricities are treasured and respected by all."

Shay could feel the vibrations of Dag's deep laugh against her back, and she was unable to hold back a grin as he kissed her cheek and said, "Oh, they must love you! You're wild enough to keep the whole town buzzing and amused from one year to the next."

"Nonsense!" she exclaimed, giving him a retaliatory pinch on the thigh. "I'm just one of your average emancipated Yankee ladies. If you take a close look around, you'll find slews of us all over New England."

"Hah! Average, my foot. Just like your average temper, and your average sexy body, to say nothing of those average eyes and that average hair. Hmmmmmm...speaking of your body..."

With a move worthy of Houdini, Dag's hands were somehow under her tee-shirt and closing over her breasts.

"Dag!" Her protest started as a squeal, which turned rapidly to a breathless groan. "Reardon will be coming back...you can't...*Dag!*"

"Shhh...relax, sweetheart. We'll hear the truck. Why are you wearing this ridiculous, tight bra? Bad as breastplates. Ah, at least it has a front catch."

"Ohhh...don't, you beast." Even as she protested, Shay knew it was halfhearted, to say the least. Although she grabbed his wrists, she didn't even try to pull the warm hands and teasing fingers away. If anything, she urged him on as she felt the aching fullness of her breasts pressing into his palms and her nipples hardening to taut peaks under the light brushing of his fingers.

The repeated shocks of the past hours had put Shay in a highly strung emotional state, and that, coupled with the explosive chemistry between her and Dag, sent her right over the edge. She jerked her knees up, thighs pressing tightly together, as a passionate need flamed through her, fogging her mind and spreading a hot, moist weakness through her loins.

Dag, whose main thought had no doubt been to distract her mind from recent horrors, suddenly found his arms and hands full of a moaning, panting, twisting wild woman.

Neither of them retained the least sense of where they were. Their instincts were totally involved with getting as close to each other as possible. She pulled, he pushed, and they were on the ground, the hot, frenzied, open-mouthed kiss unbroken, her legs entwined around his, her hands digging into his tight buttocks and urging him on in the rhythmic motion that had her arching her back and moaning a wordless plea.

It wasn't until Dag raised up on one elbow and reached for the snap on her jeans that the first glimmer of intelligent awareness broke through Shay's state of passionate mindlessness. Dag, too, brought his head up and his attention back to their surroundings.

"Oh, no, sweetheart, *not* like this." In one smooth, continuous move, he rolled back up onto his knees, wrapping his hands around Shay's waist and pulling her up to a sitting position at the same time. He shifted his hands to cup her face, shaking her head gently from side to side. "Come on, Valkyrie, snap out of it. That's my girl."

He sat back, facing her as the hectic flush of color receded from her cheeks and her blaze of passion died out. Letting his hands slide slowly down her arms until he could grasp her hands, he explained, "Not that I don't want you. You know I do. But another minute of that and young Reardon would have had the Shay-story of the year to tell."

"Wouldn't he just!" Shay agreed, still getting her breath back. She looked up at him as he knelt in front of her, and said in her usual forthright manner, "I don't understand this weird affect you have on me. I've never attacked a man in my life before. It's not funny," she admonished as he grinned at her. "Every time you get near me, boom! I go up like a rocket, and I don't like it at all."

Dag laughed aloud at her peeved expression. "We'll debate that later, sweetness. I think this time it was more a matter of reacting to all the death and destruction we've faced."

Tilting her head in thought, Shay said slowly, "A sort of life force drive to ensure the continuance of the race?

Hmm, maybe. The birth rate always does shoot up after wars and disasters." Her attitude changed to one of amused assessment as she challenged, "So tell me, Viking, what was the catalyst Sunday night?"

She didn't know why she was pushing it. She hadn't really wanted to admit just how strong the attraction was between them, at least not out loud, not to him. Not for a second was he going to believe that she didn't like it. It was all too obvious that she did. And there was no point in trying to convince him, or herself, that it was all due to imagination, too much wine, the low barometric pressure, the humidity, or any of the other dozen excuses she'd thought of in the past forty-eight hours. *If you had half an ounce of sense, you dumb broad, you'd drop the subject right now and discuss . . . wood stoves, and how useful all those fallen trees are going to be. Or rose gardens. Or camps for handicapped children.*

With a knowing smile that brought a flash to her eyes, Dag said, "You know damn well what it was. However, we are not going to discuss it now. I've got a much better site in mind for a friendly debate on the subject. Later. When we can be sure of no interruptions. And when you don't have so many potential weapons lying about in arm's reach."

Following the direction of his sweeping scan of the area, Shay burst into a peal of laughter as she noted the number of club-sized branches and boards scattered about.

Before she had time to comment, Dag poured another cup of soup and resolutely changed the subject. "Here, have some of this while it's still hot. You hardly tasted it before, and you still need it."

He hesitated a few moments while she sipped cautiously at the soup, and then he said slowly, "I can understand if you don't want to talk about it, but . . . I've been wondering . . . you're so . . . independent and strong . . . I mean in the sense of strength of character . . . and—Oh, hell, what I don't understand is why you stayed married to Severin for so long, considering the way he treated you. Why didn't you get a divorce, or at least a legal separation so the courts could protect your interests?"

Leaning back against the tree trunk again, Shay stared

pensively into the soup cup while she searched for the right words to explain a seemingly illogical situation.

"Stubbornness," she said at last. "Some people might call it an excess of pride, but I truly think it was just plain old-fashioned bullheadedness. When things started to go wrong, which was almost from the beginning, I simply refused to admit that I could have been so stupid and so lacking in judgment. Then, for a long time, maybe four or five years, I was bound and determined that I was going to hang in there and somehow make it work. I fought every step of the way, trying to force Cary to recognize his responsibility to the boys, if not to me. It took a long time before I admitted that you simply can't change a person's basic nature."

She drank some of the soup and handed Dag the cup to share as she continued, "I've done a lot of thinking about it all in the last few years—since I've been back here. Distance and time really do lend perspective, and I'm sure now that I was as wrong for Cary as he was for me. Oh, he was weak and self-centered. There's no question that he didn't want the responsibility for a family—didn't even want a family, in fact. But other men have found themselves in that situation, and somehow they've managed to cope. I wonder if Cary would have, too, if I'd been a different kind of woman. Perhaps if I'd been fragile, feminine, and dependent, it would have stroked his masculine ego enough to—"

A sound that could only be described as a snort interrupted her musing. Startled, she turned to Dag and caught her breath at the blatant sexuality in the assessing examination he was making of her seventy-one inches. When his eyes finally met hers, she felt her hackles rising at the possessive gleam he was making no attempt to hide.

Before she could voice a protest he announced, in much the tone of a royal decree, "*I* think you're perfectly splendid and feminine just the way you are—temper, independence, and all. I've had all the fluttery, fragile featherwits I could tolerate and, believe me, a man can take just so much of that without OD-ing on blandness. Furthermore, *my* masculine ego is in fine shape. I can think of much more interesting things for you to stroke."

Shay stiffened in alarm as his eyes locked with hers and

she saw the flicker of hot anticipation in his compelling gaze. She also saw his widening smile as he noted her wariness. For the something-thousandth time, she cursed her all-too-expressive eyes that had always made it impossible for her to hide her thoughts or feelings.

If my eyes are reflecting the state of my mind, they're spinning in concentric circles. Why, why does this man affect me so? He probably wouldn't come on half as strong if he knew just how inexperienced I really am. He probably thinks I—

Dag's finger tapping her cheek brought her attention back to him, and she wondered why he was suddenly scowling.

"What did he do to you?" he demanded.

"Do to me?" Shay repeated in confusion. "I don't know what you mean. He left me—"

"No, I'm not talking about that. I mean physically, sexually, something."

"Now just wait one minute," she yelped indignantly. "That's none of your business! I don't even talk to my mother about . . . that is, there wasn't anything . . . he didn't . . . we hardly ever . . . I mean, it wasn't all that . . ."

Shay trailed off into an incoherent sputter, her eyes widening again in alarm as she saw Dag's expression change from confusion to startled understanding.

She couldn't stand it. Her brows drew together in a ferocious scowl, and the angry, incautious words erupted before she realized what she was giving away. "You can just stop looking at me like that, dammit? You don't know anything! It didn't matter a bit. I didn't care anyhow. The whole subject is highly overrated, and I don't believe half the—"

"Hah! I should've guessed from the way you respond to me. Such a beautifully passionate reaction, and then that look you get of sheer amazement as if you'd never—"

"Don't be ridiculous! I've got two children! Of course, I've—"

"Hush, sweetheart," he crooned, touching her mouth with silencing fingertips. His demeanor was a mixture of gleeful satisfaction, awe, and something deeper, which Shay wasn't yet ready to interpret. "That's it, isn't it? Even the most inept lover can get a woman pregnant, and he was inept, wasn't he? No, don't shake your head at me. I'm right. I should have figured it out sooner. A lovely, passionate woman in her prime years who's content to do without sexual involvement—it was that flaming independence that threw me off. Of course he didn't abuse you—you'd have handed him his head and—"

"I'll hand you your head in a minute," Shay snarled wrathfully.

"Don't get upset, honey. It's not your fault the guy was a lousy lover. As a matter of fact," he said slowly with a pleased, seductive smile, "I could almost thank the idiot."

Shay stared at him. She parted her lips but then couldn't think of what to say. She wasn't even quite sure how she felt at that moment. Anger, yes. He had no business digging into the intimate details of her marriage. Embarrassment and chagrin, definitely. There was something ludicrous, if not absolutely farcical, about a thirty-two-year-old widow who had never experienced sexual fulfillment—especially in this day and age. Oh, she knew what it was theoretically, but descriptions in books had little to do with Cary's hurried couplings. Never had he made her feel a hundredth of the excitement, need, arousal, that this determined Viking did. How had he known? And why did it please him?

She was so involved in trying to work out logical answers to the dozens of questions spinning in her mind that she forgot to protest when Dag drew her into his arms. Holding her loosely, he stroked calming hands over her back.

"I really could, you know," he murmured.

"What?"

"Thank him for messing you up."

"That's an awful thing to say!" Shay exclaimed, staring reproachfully into the teasing eyes only inches away. The inches disappeared as he dropped a light kiss on her jutting lower lip.

"Not from my viewpoint, sweetheart. If he hadn't turned you off men so thoroughly, you wouldn't have been here waiting for me."

"Waiting for you!" Shay tried to push him away, but she gained no more than an inch or so before she felt his hands lock behind her back. "I haven't been waiting for you or any other man. I'm perfectly capable—"

"Of course you are, my darling firecracker. On the other hand, you have to admit that you really don't know what you've been missing."

"Of all the arrogant—"

"No, not arrogant. Just truthful," he murmured absently.

Shay tried to decipher his bemused expression, wondering what had distracted his attention. Her speculations were cut short as his mouth widened in a slow, sensual smile and his eyes sparked with promise. Resigned, she waited for his next outrageous remark.

"I've just realized," he said in a tone somewhere between awe and delight, "that it will be the next best thing to being the first."

"I don't want to know what you're talking about," she said repressively, trying unsuccessfully to push him further away.

"Teaching you to—" Dag broke off at the sound of the truck engine.

Shay scrambled to her feet, muttering, "Nice timing, Reardon." She quickly stepped out into plain sight.

"Coward," Dag murmured, moving up beside her. "It won't go away by ignoring it, you know. You should also know by now that all men are not alike."

She couldn't resist. Nearly choking with the effort to suppress her laughter, Shay stepped back and gave him a long, assessing examination. Copying his earlier appraisal of herself, she carefully scanned his long, athletic legs, lean hips, broad shoulders, and handsome face. She let her gaze linger for a moment on his close-cropped platinum curls before she finally met his amused look.

Letting a grin break loose at last, she purred, "They certainly aren't."

"I dare you to do that when we're not about to be interrupted," he drawled, swinging her around and starting them both moving toward the truck.

It was nearly nine o'clock that evening before Shay and Dag finally left the roads and went to get a few hours of much needed sleep. Throughout the afternoon and evening, truckloads and planeloads of rescue workers and emergency equipment had been pouring into the five-state area. At last, by mid-evening, all of those who had been working almost nonstop for over eighteen hours were relieved and sent off to rest.

The roads into Beech Village were still not clear, so Dag headed for the inn. Shay was too tired to make more than a token protest. She didn't really care where he took her at that point as long as it resulted in a shower and a bed.

Dag parked the truck at the far end of the inn's south wing next to an outside staircase that led up to his private suite. Shay was so tired she was swaying on her feet, and Dag kept his arm around her as he urged her up the steps.

"Hang in, sweetheart. Just a few more minutes and you can sleep for the next ten hours."

"Best idea anyone's had all day," she muttered, leaning against him while he unlocked the door.

She didn't really take in the small hallway or the pleasant sitting room. It wasn't until Dag paused in the doorway of the bedroom to flip the light switch that Shay finally opened her eyes wide—and then widened them even more as she stared incredulously at the immense bed that seemed to fill at least two-thirds of the room.

"Good grief," she said faintly. "You went right by king-sized and straight to super-dynastic. If you put a couple of kids head to toe across the bottom, you could sleep a family of eight in there. Or two families of four. Or all three bears *and* little old Goldilocks."

"You've really had it, sweetheart," Dag soothed between chuckles. "You're beginning to babble."

She had to agree with him. As she watched the laughing brown eyes coming closer, and with her mind filled with an indelible vision of the huge bed, she had the distinct feeling that reality was somehow slipping out of her grasp.

Tomorrow . . . tomorrow I'll set him straight. Tonight I just want to sleep. In that lovely great bed. And if he wants to lend me his chest to lean against, so what. I'm too tired to argue about it, and besides, it feels good. Oh, Shay, you're going to regret this. But not until tomorrow, and tomorrow I'll make sure he understands. Besides, what's to worry about? Neither of us has the energy for fun and games. He's just as exhausted as I am. By the time I wake up, I'll be in shape to handle him. And don't think he doesn't know that, you dumb twit, but do you believe for one minute that his ideas on being handled are the same as yours? Oh, shut up.

It was the last coherent thought she had. She could feel exhaustion swamping her senses, and she nearly cried from frustration when her fingers refused to obey her as she tried to undress. She was only dimly aware that the hands stripping off her clothes weren't her own, but some vestige of sense surfaced when the strong arms supporting her tried to urge her toward the bed.

"Shower," she mumbled, and she felt the vibration of a chuckle in the bare chest pressed against her back.

It was the sound of his voice rather than the words that she heard as he urged, encouraged, and scolded her into the shower and kept her on her feet until they were both scrubbed clean. She did manage to mutter "Hair" at some point, and then felt Dag pull her arms around his neck.

"Don't let go, Shay. I need both hands for this."

The sharpness of the command got through to her, and she tightened her arms, leaning the full length of her body against his, thinking vaguely how nice it felt to be naked with him. Drifting in and out of a light doze, she obeyed his hands and voice. Afterwards, all she could remember was a foggy recollection of his fingers massaging her scalp, the softness of a towel on her body, the warmth of blowing air on her hair, and his breathless laugh and the words, "Just a few steps, sweetheart. I'm in no shape to carry you right now."

chapter 10

Ummm . . . tickles . . . what's on my bottom? Hands? Big hands . . . very big hands . . . Marcus? Can't be . . . loving your mother is one thing; rubbing her butt is another. He can't possibly have that kind of problem. Oooooo . . . nice . . . too nice. Who are you kidding, mush mind? How can anything that feels so good be too nice? Oh, hush. I've figured it out . . . it's all a dream . . . too much sublimating and then that man stirring me all up . . . no wonder I'm having erotic fantasies . . . him and his damn Valkyries and breast-plates . . . no, we decided to skip the breastplates. Snap out of it, girl, this is no dream. Those are real hands stroking your legs. Nonsense! Oh! What—? He couldn't have! Oh, but he did, sleeping beauty, and if you don't want to get nipped on the other side, you'd better wake up right quick. But—But nothing. Check the state of your innards, girl. He's already got you halfway to spontaneous combustion. Don't be ridic— . . . he? . . . he who? Idiot! He who has you squirming all over the bed. He who is running his tongue up the inside of your thigh. He who belongs to those magical fingers that are—

"Dag! Omilord, what . . . what do you think you're doing?" Shay croaked as she lunged up from where she had been sleeping on her stomach and half twisted around to stare in dazed fascination at the naked Viking kneeling between her legs.

He kissed the sensitive spot at the back of her knee before raising his head to look at her face. "Rousing you from sleep, sweetheart." His sherry eyes fairly sizzled as his gaze dropped to the firm profile of her breasts with their tight, dark nipples. "Or *a*rousing you?"

His voice and smile were equally seductive, and Shay's eyes widened in a mixture of alarm and excitement. Desperately, she tried to corral her disoriented, swirling thoughts and get herself and this impossible situation under control. Her nervous system felt like it was shorting out under the strain of sending so many signals so fast to her fuzzy brain. Not that it was achieving much. Her mind was rapidly losing the battle for coherent thought, and was succumbing to the white heat surging through her and melting every vestige of resistance. She couldn't believe this was happening to her. Never before...

Bewilderedly, she reached out a questing hand, and he leaned forward so she could touch his hair. Her fingers wound into his curls, and she stared as if she'd never seen hair before as he dropped his head to kiss her hip. Her gaze drifted past the platinum pelt and fixed curiously on the long fingers that were gently playing in the thick curly tangle of flame silk at the joining of her thighs. It took several long seconds before her overheating mind connected those clever fingers with the hot, moist unfurling in her loins. She felt drugged as she slowly brought her questioning eyes up to meet his waiting gaze.

"Dag?" It was a whisper, full of disbelief, wonder, curiosity, and burgeoning joy.

For a timeless moment everything was suspended except for the slow threading of his fingers in her soft curls and their uneven breathing.

"Oh, sweetheart, you great gorgeous gift from the gods." His voice was husky with restrained passion and excitement, and an exultant light flashed in his eyes.

It was too much. Shay closed her eyes, trying to hold back the hot honey-sweet spell he was weaving around and through her, but his hands moving on her legs and hips, turning her, spreading her, totally banished her last wisp of resistance. The touch of his mouth nibbling kisses up across her belly and his hands sliding over her ribs to close around her breasts brought her eyes open again, and she ran her hands over the taut, smooth skin of his shoulders, digging her fingers into his muscles as his lips began discovering the firm curves of her breasts.

She was functioning purely on an instinctive level. No thoughts, no doubts, no questions, no protests had a chance to penetrate her hazy mind. Her long-denied libido was sending imperative messages to her reflexes, and somewhere deep inside, her suppressed female appetites and craving for fulfillment finally rocketed out of her control and sent waves of searing heat through every tissue of her body.

Need. She needed something. He was driving her mad with his mouth and his hands and the softness of his hair brushing, brushing back and forth. It was too much, what he was doing with his mouth and his tongue, but it wasn't enough and there was something more she needed to fill that aching pulsing flexing emptiness. More and more, and her arms were empty and she wanted to hold on to him, feel all of him against her, in her, moving, now, now, now and now it was everything she'd wanted and never known and it was so much more than she would have believed.

Instincts sent the pillows flying out of the way, brought her arms and legs tightly around him as he lost his own control and drove into her waiting depths. Instincts arched her back and moved her hips in a strong, twisting counter-rhythm, made her head thrash back and forth, whipping her long hair around them in a flaming tangle. Instincts forced the inarticulate moans and cries from her throat, curved her fingers into a bruising grip on the tight muscles of his buttocks and brought her hips surging up to meet his as he locked his arms around her and drove them both over the edge into a roaring, spinning, tumbling maelstrom that whirled them through a spiral of psychedelically flashing lights and out into blackness . . .

The only sounds in the room were chorusing birds and the harsh pants of laboring lungs. The only movements were the gentle flutter of the curtains at the open windows, and the slow sliding of Shay's legs down over his hips to rest across the backs of his thighs, the relaxing of her arms as they dropped away from him until just her hands lay lightly against his waist, and after a few minutes, the shifting of Dag's arms as he pulled them out from beneath her back and tucked his elbows in beside hers to take some of his weight off of her. He slid his hands under the outer curves of her shoulders and gently stroked his fingers back and forth, while his breathing gradually slowed to normal. Shay was still, a boneless, mindless heap, and the effort to so much as twitch an eyelash was completely beyond her.

Dag's head rested next to hers, cushioned on her hair, his face turned so his lips lightly touched her neck. Strands of brilliant red drifted across his shoulders and neck and mingled with his silver curls. For a while Shay was content to float, letting her mind take its own sweet time to start functioning again.

"Shay?" he whispered against her neck.

She was cocooned in plushy, golden-glowing velvet, and she was aware of only two feelings: an enervating languor and astonishment. Dag had to repeat her name twice before a tiny glimmer of current awareness forced its way into her consciousness.

"Mmmm?"

"Are you all right?"

"Mmmm . . ."

"Shay?"

"Mmmm?"

"Am I too heavy? Maybe I should—"

"Uh uh." She pressed her hands against his waist, stopping his halfhearted effort to rise.

"Are you sure?"

"Ikewareare."

"What? Sweetheart, you're not making sense."

"Am. Like you where you are," she articulated carefully.

Dag leaned up on his forearms so he could look down at her face. "Ah, sweet Valkyrie, I do love that expression— like a cat who's just found an acre of wild catnip."

Shay's lashes finally wafted upwards, and she murmured, "Are you trying to tell me you're a weed? Or warn me that you're uncultivated? Uncivilized? A barbarian, perhaps? For instance, a Viking raider?"

"I should have known you'd get back to that," he sighed,

essaying an unconvincingly mournful look. "Just remember, you were more than eager to fall into my bed last night. In fact, I couldn't keep you out of it."

"Too true. On the other hand, I don't recall anything after being in the shower, so how did I get here? Never say you carried me!"

Dag's teeth flashed white against his tan in a mock apologetic smile. "My darling, believe that I love you just the way you are, all seventy-one glorious inches of you, and try to understand that last night I was in no shape to get you off the ground, never mind carry you anywhere."

He bent his head to kiss her lightly, but she flicked her tongue across his lips and brought one hand up to hold his head in place. Slowly, intently, they explored each other's mouths, and she felt that delicious pressure building again deep inside as he began to react to their kiss and her questing hand that was adventuring over his back and hips. There were questions she wanted to ask him; but within a very few minutes she decided that serious discussions could wait until later. Much later.

"Sweetness? Are you sure you're all right? In another minute, it's going to be—"

"Just tell me, Viking, can you make me feel like that again?"

"Believe it. Again and again and again."

"Ahhhh, then I couldn't be splendider."

"Splendider?"

"Oh, yes, and wonderfuller and marvelouser and fantasticker and—"

"Valkyrie, my darling Valkyrie, you'll be all of that and more so. This is just the beginning. Tell me again, a hundred sunrises from now."

"Truly?"

"Oh, yes . . ."

"Oooohhh . . . yeeessss . . ."

chapter 11

SHAY STRETCHED, REACHING for the sky, until every muscle unkinked, then she abruptly doubled over at the waist and brushed her knuckles against the grass. She straightened up and walked toward the redwood picnic table where Dag sat watching her. Avoiding his amused eyes, she concentrated on tucking her bright blue tee-shirt into her jeans and wishing heartily that her mother had not seen fit to pack this particular shirt with its announcement that "Parsley Makes You Sexy" emblazoned across the front. Dag had greeted its appearance that morning with a murmured, "Maybe we should replace half the catnip with parsley," accompanied by a decidedly lascivious grin.

As Shay sat down across the table from him, Dag reached into the large styrofoam cooler beside him for a can of apple juice.

"Here, love, you'll feel much better after a cold drink."

"I feel fine," Shay protested, nevertheless reaching eagerly for the chilled can. "What have we got left in there to eat? I'm starved."

Dag started taking containers and wrapped sandwiches from the cooler and setting them out on the table. For a few moments Shay's attention wandered to their surroundings. The picnic table, a little cracked and battered, was all that was left of a once-pretty roadside park, which was now a tangle of uprooted trees, broken redwood planks, and mangled trash cans. They'd set the salvaged table up under one of the few remaining upright trees, and Shay sighed with relief to be out of the glare of the late afternoon sun.

Dag heard the sigh and gave her a concerned look. "Tired, sweetheart?"

"A little." She leaned her cheek against an upraised fist and finally met his eyes. "It's been a long day." She managed not to smile, but her eyes glinted with an answering amusement as she added, "But no tireder than you."

He peeled the top off a plastic container of marinated tomato and cucumber slices, stuck a fork into it, and pushed it across the table.

As she reached for it, he caught and held her eyes with a probing look and asked softly, "Are you ready to talk about things now?"

She tore her gaze away and stared at the jumble of red and pale green in the container, idly mixing the slices around in the marinade. Was she ready to talk? They were going to have to sometime. She'd held him off that morning with light banter and the need to hurry. It had been past seven-thirty by the time they'd reluctantly let go of each other and gotten up. There'd been time for little more than quick showers, a mad scramble to find clean clothes, and a hurried breakfast. Except for those few moments just before they left his suite.

They were at the door when Dag turned and cupped her face between his hands. His eyes had been...assessing, intent, as they examined her expression, and she knew that he was seeing the confusion of amazement, fulfillment, barely banked passion, apprehension, and all the other things she was feeling—including something she wasn't yet ready to identify.

"Oh, sweetheart, don't look like that. It's all so very simple. Don't you understand?"

"I'm not sure. I think...it never...I never...that was so...oh, hell!" she choked, burying her face in the curve of his neck and wrapping her arms around his waist.

He rubbed her back, kissed her behind the ear, and said soothingly, "Poor darling, it's all hitting you at once, and so much more than you expected."

"How . . . do you know?" she whispered, going very still.

"What it was like for you? Unlike some people, I haven't been living in a sexual desert for the past umpteen years. Not that I'm really objecting that you have. In fact," he purred, tipping her head back so he could see her face, "I'm positively joyful that you've saved it all for me."

It was a deliberate provocation, and he laughed and jumped nimbly backwards as she tried to shove him away from her.

"You smug, arrogant, impossible . . . witch! Warlock! Oh, whatever! I swear you cast spells!"

"Was I right about sunrises?"

"What?" Shay glared at him in confusion.

"Sunrises. Remember what I told you?"

"Oh, that. Yes." Her eyes softened with recent, vivid memories, and her lips twitched in a reluctant smile. "Oh, damn you, you Norse know-it-all. Yes, you were right."

"Shay—"

"No, not now. I . . . I need to think, and there isn't time now. Can't we wait and talk later?" she asked with a touch of desperation.

He gave her a long analytical look, and, with a smile reminiscent of a wolf eyeing a particularly succulent lamb, he conceded magnanimously, "Of course we can talk later, sweetheart. Any time you're ready. It shouldn't take all that long to get things settled, but we've got a busy day, so it'll be just as well to wait until we can relax and take our time."

With that enigmatic pronouncement, he opened the door with a flourish and swept her out and down to breakfast. Shay, exercising rare restraint, did no more than give him a sharp glare, and then spent the rest of the day avoiding any subject that might lead to a discussion of their relationship.

The definition of that relationship, if indeed they had one, occupied her mind at odd moments throughout the day. Several times, as she recalled in explicit detail Dag's method of welcoming the sunrise, she felt her body suffuse with heat and knew that her face was flushed. Wary of his apparent ability to read her mind at the most embarrassing moments, she tried to avoid being near him when her thoughts strayed to that incredible awakening.

It had helped that they'd been very busy all day in the

ongoing effort to get the main roads completely cleared and to open up at least one unobstructed lane on the secondary roads. Now, however, they were finished for the day, and she had evidently run out of thinking time.

Not that I've actually thought about decisions or relationships or how I'm going to handle him. Mmmm . . . I know how I'd like to handle—Shay! Enough! That's all you've had on your mind all day. And why not? I've finally, at last, years late, found out just what the hell everybody's always raving about. Ooooooo, did I ever find out! For heaven's sake, you sound like a sex-starved—Listen, sensible self, I am sex-starved and have been for years and was all the time I was married. I didn't even know how much I'd missed until this morning. And now that you do, where are you planning to go from here? A sneaky little affair? No! I mean, I haven't figured it out. Maybe I'll wait and see what he wants. You feeble-minded twit! It's perfectly clear what he wants, and it's not just a few nights in bed with you. Haven't you been listening to him, or seen that mine-all-mine look in his eye? Your days are numbered, old girl. Don't be ridiculous! He doesn't have any idea of getting tied down with an oversized widow and two half-grown kids. Oh, no? NO!

"Shay?"

"Mmm?"

"Do you want to talk now?"

"I . . . ah . . . guess so. What did you . . . ?"

"It's obvious, isn't it? After this morning?"

"What . . . what about this morning? I mean, I know it was—"

"It was the first time it ever happened for you. We've already agreed on that, haven't we?"

"Well . . . yes, I guess so."

"Don't scowl at me, darling. You'll have me thinking you didn't like it as much as I know damn well you did."

"Oh, you're impossible! All right. All right! I liked it. It was incredible, fantastic, and, as the boys would say, awesome. There. I've admitted it. So, what else is there to discuss?"

"Where would you like to start? Oh, sweet Shay, tuck

that lip in. Come on, now, we really should make some plans."

"What . . . kind . . . of plans?"

"Let's see . . . there's setting a wedding date . . . and then we'll have to figure out how to get some time to ourselves—"

"What wedding date?"

"Calm down, sweetheart. Just sit down there and close your mouth before birds nest in it. Our wedding date. You didn't think—"

"You are totally, utterly, certifiably, unquestionably mad, mad, mad."

". . . I was just toying with your affections, did you? What kind—"

"Why are you running around loose? Isn't somebody—"

". . . of a guy do you think I am? I'd never think of—"

"I know what it is—you were reincarnated. You were one of those beserk Vikings, and you got whammed on the head with a battle-axe. It scrambled your brains, and no one unscrambled them before—"

". . . trifling with a bad-tempered widow-lady with two kids. Especially when she's almost as big as I am. And has such lovely legs and beautiful breasts and goes absolutely wild when—"

"I am *not* bad-tempered!"

". . . I make love to her. Please, sweetheart, not the chicken salad. It's so hard to get out mayonnaise stains. Now, I understand how excited you must be. After all, it's been quite a while since you've had a proposal, but do try—"

"I've had several proposals. So there."

". . . to quiet down long enough to decide when we can get married."

"July 33, 1998."

"Hmmm . . . that won't do, I'm afraid. I've really got my heart set on having my very own Valkyrie before the weather gets cold. It's almost impossible to find decent wolfskins these days, and—"

"I'll give you an electric blanket for Christmas. I'm not getting married."

"Why not?"

"Because . . . because . . ."

"Well? Are you afraid I'll let you down? I'm not a Cary Severin, you know. I'm loyal, trustworthy, home-loving, dependable—"

"So's a Boy Scout!"

"Ah, but a Boy Scout couldn't pleasure you half as well as I can, and you won't find one that's anywhere near up to your weight in a fight. Just think how boring it is to be sizzling mad and not have anyone brave enough or big enough to give you a good battle. And then there's the making up. There hasn't been a Boy Scout born who could cope with you in a night-long reconciliation. You really are something else, my sweet Valkyrie. I can't wait until you've passed the beginner's course, and we can get on with—"

"Oh, you . . . you Casanova! Stop purring at me. There's more to marriage than sex. What do you mean, beginner's course?"

"I'll explain the curriculum tonight. I can't really do it justice across a picnic table. As far as marriage goes, we definitely have a lot more going for us than sex. We have—"

"Tonight? What do you mean, tonight? I'm not—"

"Yes, you are. They still haven't got the roads clear into the village. Didn't you hear Brady?"

"But—"

"Where else would you stay but with me? If you're honest, you have to admit that you really want to."

"Dag . . ."

"Aren't you the least bit curious about lesson two?"

"Lesson two? What's lesson two?"

"That's what's on the agenda for tonight. Trust me, sweetheart, you'll love it. Now, to get back to our wedding date, how about—"

"Dammit! Be reasonable, you Norse noodle. We've only known each other for three days. Three days!"

"Four. I don't believe in making hasty decisions, and I always said I'd never propose to a woman I'd known less than four days. Sunday, Monday, Tuesday, and this is Wednesday. Four days. So, when are you going to marry me?"

"Ohmigod, I don't believe this. That hurricane knocked out your common sense along with half the trees in New

England. Think, man. I've got two kids and a mother. We're a package deal."

"I'm mad about your boys, and your mother's a darling."

"You say I've got a terrible temper."

"I love fighting with you. Besides, once we're living together and making love every night, you won't have either the energy or the desire to lose your temper more than once a week. Just often enough to keep things interesting."

"Promises, promises . . ."

"Guaranteed."

"I won't be dominated."

"Have I tried? It's not necessary, anyhow. I know better ways to get around you. Much more fun, too, than trying to force you into going my way."

"Oh, yeah? How?"

"Mmmmm . . . so far, I've discovered that stroking your beautiful butt makes you purr, kissing your breasts makes you moan for more, and once I'm inside you, you'd agree to anything I asked—except by then I'm beyond thinking up silly questions."

"Oh . . . you . . . oh!"

"Any more objections?"

"Dozens! I don't care what anyone says about a woman going where her husband goes. I love Beech Village and—"

"No problem. So do I. Next?"

"I'm not the little homemaker type and—"

"I can afford to hire a housekeeper. Besides, I have other plans for you. Next?"

"I'm independent. I think for myself, and I'm not—What plans?"

"That's okay. I love your rather kinky thought processes, and I've never cared for clinging vines. Just think how dull it would be if we agreed on everything. After all, there's a limit, unfortunately, to how much time we can spend horizontally. It's nice to know that we'll have lots to talk about in between making love. Next?"

"You didn't say what plans."

"First things first, sweetheart. Let's get all your objections out of the way, and then we'll discuss the future. Now, what else?"

"We . . . I . . . there's . . . it's too soon!"

"I'll agree that it was pretty fast, but sometimes it happens that way. I think I knew the minute I saw you across that parking lot, but I wanted to be sure so I took my time. I didn't decide for certain until I saw you and the boys courting mother-son hernias and group pneumonia the next morning. Why did you think I was so mad?"

"Oh, Dag, you are . . . I don't know what. Impossible! The whole thing is just impossible. I can't—"

"Just answer one question, sweet Shay. Do you love me?"

"I . . . love . . ."

"I'll even give you a clue, my reluctant Valkyrie. Think about this morning."

"Ohhh . . . that's not fair."

"Mmmm . . . I know. But since I can't hit you over the head and cart you off to my longboat, I have to use the weapons at hand. My, you certainly are remembering. If you keep looking at me like that, you're going to have lesson two right under this table. God, I love your eyes, especially when they get that hot, hungry look."

"They don't!"

"Oh, lady fox, they do, they do. Why can't you say 'I love you'? You did this morning."

"I—This morning? When?"

"The second time. Mmmm . . . maybe you don't remember . . . you *were* getting rather wild about then. It was just before you bit my shoulder, or was it—"

"I never!"

"You did, you know. Want to see the teethmarks? I may borrow Dan's Polaroid tonight and have you take a picture of them. We could frame it and hang it in our bedroom and—"

"Dag!"

". . . call it 'Shay's Awakening' or perhaps—"

"Will you stop? Anyway, what are you fussing about? I've got bruises all over me."

"I'll bet you have, sweetheart. You're a wild woman once you're turned on, and it takes some doing to keep you where I want you. I've probably got just as many bruises as you have, you know. You've got very strong hands for a woman. Not that I mind, darling. It was—"

"Oooohhhh . . ."

"Stop chewing your braid, love. It won't be long now. When we get back to the inn, we'll take a shower and compare battle scars. Sweet Shay, I'll kiss all your bruises better if you'll do the same for me, and then we can—"

"Ummmf!"

"No, don't hide your face. It's too late. Did you know that blush clashes with your hair?"

"Nemimyhar."

"You're getting incoherent again, darling, or is it because you've got your fist in your mouth? Come on, sweetheart, look at me and tell me how soon we can be married. Please? Or do you have some more objections?"

"I . . . it's . . . oh, stop looking at me with that smarmy grin!"

"Please, love. Smarmy? Not a bit of it. That's affection. I really do love you, Shay MacAllister. And your sons and your mother and your village and your house and everything about you. Just the way you are. I wouldn't change a thing. Now, you can't possibly have any more objections."

"Don't bet on it!"

"Aahh hah! What a terrific idea! A bet! How's your sporting blood, love? Let's see, we need a time limit. Two weeks should be enough, and then we can be married on the Saturday after Labor Day, and—"

"Wait! Just wait a minute, you madman. What are you talking about? What bet? I haven't—"

"What else do we need? Mmmm? Terms, we need to specify the terms. I'll bet that within two weeks from today I can get you to say 'yes' to marrying me."

"Don't be ridiculous! I'm not—"

"I'm betting you will. Stakes. What shall we use for stakes? What do you say, Shay my sweet? How sure are you that you can hold out?"

"I don't like that gleam in your eye, Viking. You're up to something."

"Perhaps . . . well, if you think you'll give in within a couple of days, I guess we could keep the stakes low. Ah, how about if we bet a dinner? Loser buys. Or—"

"I'm not going to give in! Dammit, I won't have my

future decided on a dumb bet for a dinner!"

"You're right, a Valkyrie is worth much more than a dinner. And, of course, we should keep in mind that famous pigheadedness of yours. There's always the chance that I can't bring you around in two weeks. Now that I really consider it, you just might win."

"Damn right! You can bet on it."

"I'm trying to. Well, if you're that sure you can win, let's make the stakes interesting. If I lose, you get . . . what do you want?"

"Um . . . oh, I know! Dinner for four, for Mother, the boys and me, at the inn once a week for the next six months. Or is that too much?"

"Nothing is too much if it makes you smile like that. And if you lose, what are you offering?"

"I know I'm going to regret this, but . . . what do you want? No! Wait a minute. If I lose, that means I've agreed to marry you, so you get me!"

"Wrong, darling. The stakes have to be separate from the bet. Hmmm . . . what do I want that you have—besides your delectable self, that is? Aaahhh, land. I could use some land around here if it's the right kind. What are those pieces of land you mentioned?"

"Land! What do you—Oh, all right. There's one chunk, about fifty acres, that's down along the Connecticut River. We lease it to a market gardener, but—"

"Uh uh. That won't do. What else?"

"What else . . . ah . . . there's a little over seventy acres outside New Salem. It's the last of a big tract the Mac-Allisters owned in the Swift River Valley. The rest was bought by the state when they did the land-takings for the Quabbin Reservoir in the nineteen-thirties. We—"

"Nope. Too far away. Is that all?"

"No, there's—"

"Have you got anything closer to Beech Village?"

"Well . . . yes . . . but . . . I can't imagine what you'd want with so much unless—Are you thinking of building another inn?"

"No. Tell me about this land."

"It's two hundred and ten acres. A mixture of meadowland, pasture, woods, some high granite ridges, and there's a pure, spring-fed brook and a pond. It's only a few miles north of the village, but it's kind of out of the way. Most of the land in that area is abandoned. Lots of wildlife. The boys and I go camping up there once in a while."

"Sounds just right. How close is it to a paved road?"

"There's almost a hundred yards of frontage on the west end of Fallow Ridge Road. That's the road you followed me on from Route 202 to the village. It continues to the west, kind of northwest, and meets Route 63 over near Leverett."

"Perfect. That's what you can bet, sweetheart."

"Two hundred and ten acres of land?"

"I love it when you get that totally bewildered look on your face. Do you realize that right now you look about eighteen?"

"Nonsense!"

"Mmm. Listen, you can rest easy about the land. Remember, if I win, we'll be getting married so you won't really, truly be losing the land at all. Well now, I think that takes care of everything. Terms, stakes, time limit. Shall we shake on it?"

Dag held out his right hand, and Shay, with a half-wary, half-baffled expression, hesitantly took it. Not for a moment did she trust that smugly triumphant glow in his eyes or that "gotcha" smile. There was something . . .

"Mousetrapped! Dammit, you sneaky Viking! I wish I had a tape of this conversation. Somewhere, somehow, you've slickered me! I just know it!"

She leaped to her feet, almost falling backwards over the seat, as Dag threw back his head and bellowed with laughter. Gasping for breath, he managed to scramble up in time to grab her and prevent her from up-ending the cooler over his head.

"No, no, darling . . . don't . . . oh, sweetheart, you walked into it so beautifully. Easy, now, easy."

He swung her around, off-balance, and then spun her back into his arms, catching both her wrists behind her back in one large hand. Wrapping her long braid around his other hand three or four times, he pulled her head back and lowered his mouth toward hers. Stopping within a half-inch of his target, he chuckled softly and warned, "If you bite me,

I'll make you take your shower alone."

Ready to yell a protest, she was left with her mouth half-open as the absurdity of his threat penetrated her ire. Dag took quick advantage of her unintentional offer and filled her mouth with his gently exploring tongue. As soon as he felt the erotic nibble of her teeth and heard her sighing moan, he disengaged his hands and dropped them down to cup her bottom and pull her hips hard against his.

Shay's arousal, already conditioned by their lovemaking that morning, was almost as immediate as his. She locked her arms around his neck and pressed into him, squirming and rubbing her breasts against the firm contours of his chest. His guiding hands weren't really necessary; her hips set their own rhythmic pace as she took fire from the increasing pressure of his hardening manhood. Shay had never really come down from her passion-induced sunrise high, and within moments she was flaming out of control and almost rocking Dag off his feet.

"Shhh...easy, love...settle down...we'll take care of it in just a little while, I promise," he crooned in her ear as he stroked gentling hands over her arms and back and gradually put a few inches between them.

She stared at him with glazed eyes and mumbled, "I don't believe what you do to me. How could I completely forget a major highway not fifty feet away with truckloads of Guardsmen zooping by every ten minutes? If you're not casting spells, you're using hypnosis or putting funny things in my apple juice."

Her threatening scowl only made him laugh and say teasingly, "If you say yes now, I won't have to put funny things in your juice anymore."

"No," she growled.

"Good!" he responded. "It's no fun to win in a walkover. Come on, Shay-the-Stubborn, let's go home and play in the shower."

chapter 12

SHAY BROUGHT HER flittering mind back to the business at hand as she saw the Amherst Road intersection ahead. Flipping on the left directional signal, she slowed to let an oncoming car go by and then swung the truck onto the road leading home. It was a road she could have driven practically blindfolded, and her mind immediately soared off like a bumblebee, touching here and there just long enough to savor a memory before flitting on to the next one.

As might be expected of a thirty-two-year-old woman who has just spent the best part of ten hours in a long-overdue discovery of the ramifications of pleasure and passion, Shay's most vivid memories were of Dag and lessons two through eight. A catnip smile spread over her face as she remembered his growly voice saying, "There's nothing that says we have to take them in order. As far as that goes, with a bit of ingenuity we can combine a couple. Like this...sweet Shay...oh, yes, love..."

She was distracted momentarily by the sight of Mac-Callum's pine grove, which looked as if a bomb had hit it, but once she was past it, her mind drifted back to the evening before when Dag had insisted on taking a shower with her. She'd had only the vaguest memories of Tuesday evening when he'd not only showered with her but washed her hair as well. Perhaps it was that vagueness that kept her from being embarrassed about it. But last night had been another bucket of beets.

Wide awake and in the bright light of early evening, she'd hesitated to undress and blatantly stroll into the bathroom with him. An only child, she'd always had all the privacy she wanted. Even in the years of her marriage, she'd automatically scheduled baths and showers around Cary's absence, and he hadn't cared enough about indulging in lighthearted sex to entice her out of her inhibitions. Dag had quickly disabused her of her notions of what he termed "ridiculous Victorian modesty," and before she had time to do more than squeak, he had them both stripped and in the shower.

Placing her hands on his shoulders and daring her to move them on pain of being doused under an ice-cold needle-spray, he proceeded to lather her body, very slowly, from neck to thighs while he delivered a laughing lecture on the Norseman's version of *The Joy of Sex*. By the time he went down on one knee to do her legs and feet, she had relaxed enough to start asking questions about this new world he was leading her into. Feeling like a naive teenager, she was tentative at first, fumbling for euphemisms and not quite sure she should even be talking about such things with him.

"Shay, my own love," he said huskily, standing up and cupping her face in his hands, "don't you know what a gift you are? Here I am, thirty-six and in love for the first time in my life. Do you know what the odds are that at my age, after finally finding my Valkyrie, I'd also discover that I'd have the delight of teaching her about love and making love. That's not to say I wouldn't love you just as much if your marriage had been a good one. I would. But I can't deny that it was like winning my first championship trophy when I realized that you were the next thing to being untouched, and that I was going to be your first lover in so many ways."

Handing her the soap and telling her to get busy, he alternately coaxed and teased her into an explicit question-and-answer session. The combination of laughter, detailed answers to her questions, and the feel of his hard, sinewy body under her soapy, exploring hands finished building the mutual fire his ministrations to her had started. She grabbed at his shoulders for balance as he pushed her back against the wall, his large hands sliding under her bottom to lift her up on her toes and hold her undulating hips still for his entry. Her shoulders were braced against the wall, her head tipped back, and her eyes closed as she tried to capture and hold the exquisite sensations that were racing through her.

"Easy, love," he whispered hoarsely against her neck. "This isn't the place for going wild. Slowly, just enough to feel the motion. Let those lovely muscles deep inside do it for you. Oh, yes . . . beautiful . . . just like that . . . Shay, sweet Shay, don't stop . . . not yet . . ."

She was in another world, conscious only of the hard, soap-slippery body rubbing against hers, the tantalizing roughness of his mat of chest hair brushing across her taut nipples, the slight tremble in his straining thighs braced between hers and taking part of her weight as her knees weakened. She was only dimly aware of the water cascading down his back, sending a fine spray against her face, and of the cold tile against her shoulders. She scarcely heard her own harsh pants and her voice gasping his name. Everything was spiraling in, deep inside her loins, as his tightly controlled thrusts accelerated, sending her spinning in and out of the spiral until the vibrating flexures began building. Her fingers dug into the solid muscles of his shoulders, and her strong back flexed and arched, almost throwing him off balance, as she twisted and flung her hips against his in an instinctive, insistent, rhythmic beat that almost destroyed his control. She was nearly screaming with the building tension inside, but some tiny fear of falling held her back.

It was his voice in her ear, a gasping growl of "Let it go, let it all go, sweet Valkyrie. I've got you safe. Just let go and fly, Valkyrie, fly . . . now . . . now . . ." that sent her spinning into a golden, pulsating mist.

Shay lifted her head and looked around with dazed eyes. The truck was stopped at the side of the road, and she'd been leaning forward with her head resting on her hands, which were clasped in a death grip around the steering wheel. Her foot, thank heavens, was jammed firmly down on the brake pedal.

She leaned to the side to look at herself in the rearview mirror. "You blithering idiot, MacAllister," she said aloud, taking in the glaze of passion clouding her eyes. "Wasn't that the first thing you said when you saw him—'six and a half feet of trouble heading straight for you'? Did you get out of the way? Oh, no, not you, Miss Smartass. You could handle anything in pants. Shuuurr, you can. Look at you! Just thinking about what he does to you sends you right off the road!"

With a sound somewhere between a moan and a laugh, Shay leaned back and stared at the up-ended remains of a large tree six feet in front of the truck. She wriggled spasmodically, pressing into the seat, trying to subdue the tingling ache of arousal.

It didn't seem to help much. Instead it made matters worse by stirring up the memory of what came after their shower. Not that she had a very clear picture of the immediate aftermath when, guided by Dag's hands and voice, she managed to get out of the shower and fold up on the vanity bench. She remembered dreamily watching him dry off and then pulling her to her feet and briskly rubbing her down with a thick towel. It wasn't until he was leading her across the bedroom, laughing at her attempt to walk a straight line, that she became conscious of an odd happening, or rather, non-happening.

Her inhibitions had washed away in the shower, and she didn't hesitate to tug on his hand and, when he turned toward her, to give him a quick, interested once-over.

She met his amused look with a quirked eyebrow, took a deep breath, and asked, "Do you have a secret stock of parsley, or did you . . . hold off for some reason?"

He pulled her into his arms and kissed her slowly and thoroughly before answering with a smug grin, "At great expense to my nervous system and stamina, I managed to hold back. If I hadn't, my sweet, we'd probably both be lying in that shower right now with cracked skulls."

"But how can you—"

"It wasn't easy, but I kept thinking of how you're going to make it all up to me."

"Oh. Ah, how am I?"

"Like this," he whispered, his eyes suddenly blazing with passion and his face taking on a sculpted look as he pulled her down onto the bed with him.

Curious, aroused, and already conditioned to obeying his guiding hands, Shay didn't balk, as she would have that morning, when he settled on his back and maneuvered her astride his hips.

"But—"

She forgot her protest as he pulled her down on his chest, holding her head still while he kissed her dizzy and squirming.

"Mmmmm . . . that's nice . . . don't stop," he murmured against her mouth, his hands busily unbraiding and finger-combing her hair until it fell around them in a red silk tent.

"Da-a-ag . . . oh . . . please . . . let me . . ." His hands stroking her thighs were driving her wild, and she wanted—

"I don't *believe* this!" she yelled, wrapping her arms around herself and banging her forehead on the steering wheel several times. With a muttered oath that she hoped her sons didn't know, she swung out of the truck and walked around it. She stopped by an old dry stone wall and stood, fists on hips, glaring belligerently out across an empty field.

"There is more to marriage than sex," she announced to the decidedly uninterested meadow. "Even if the sex is more fantastic than I ever could have imagined. Even if I'll probably never again find a man who can make me do all those things and still want more. So he says he loves me, and he claims I said it to him. It's too soon to be sure, isn't it?"

She waited, but the long grass had no comment other than a breeze-induced ripple.

"People say those things in the throes of passion, don't they? I thought I loved Cary, but it turned out I didn't."

Shay abandoned the unresponsive field and addressed her next observation to the stone wall. "Of course, Dag isn't Cary. He's different in every way. Understanding, affectionate, strong. He was there, all the way, all through the storm and the ugliness and the dead bodies and . . . everything. That says something, doesn't it?"

A precariously balanced rock rolled off the wall, coming to a stop by her feet.

"Ah ha! It does say something. And he didn't try to hold me back or tell me what to do. Every time I needed him, if just to rest against for a minute, he was there, but he didn't nag about what women should and shouldn't do. And he does like the boys . . . and Mother . . . oh, hell!"

A big gray squirrel skittered along the top of the wall and stopped ten feet away from Shay, twitching his bushy tail and chattering at her.

"Oh, you. I'll bet you're a male. You all stick together. Yes, yes, I know I'm probably crazy and I should grab him while I can, but . . . what if . . . good God, Gertrude, you're asking advice from a squirrel and a stone wall!"

At her outraged bellow, a flock of starlings, hidden by the long grass, took noisy flight, and the squirrel disappeared as if sucked through a time warp. Shay grabbed the stone at her feet and heaved it back onto the wall, making sure it was secure. With an excess of energy and little regard for potentially crushed fingers, she proceeded to repair a dozen feet of the wall, muttering under her breath the whole time.

"Mad, mad, he's driving you mad. Right out into orbit, and the vacuum has imploded your mushy mind. He said last night was day one, and today is day two, and what is he going to do about that bet? He's plotting something. I just know it. That grin when I left should be in a plain brown wrapper. He didn't say a word about seeing me again, either, so how's he going to convince me—Oh, that devious beast! He wouldn't, would he? Make love to me until I'm damn well cross-eyed, and then . . . bam! . . . hold out until I say yes? He couldn't be that mean. After all, I didn't say I didn't want to make love—I just said I didn't want to get married. Damn him, if he tries that, I'll . . . I'll . . . I'll think of something absolutely *wicked* to do to him. Oh, Shay, you are flipping out. Go home and get some sleep. God knows, last night you did just about everything that can be done in a bed *except* sleep."

With every ounce of willpower she had, she fixed her mind firmly on how she was going to repair the veranda and the fishpond, and what she was going to do about the half-destroyed rose garden Phyllis had bemoaned when Shay talked with her early that morning. Keeping her mind resolutely on such pragmatic problems and the road in front of her, Shay headed for home. She refused to acknowledge even one tiny question about how Dag planned to win their bet, or about what her ultimate answer would be.

* * *

It was twelve minutes past six that Thursday evening, day two of their bet, when Shay discovered just how far Dag was prepared to go to win—or, at least, she thought she knew the full extent of his devious, clever, not to say fiendish, plan.

It had been after one before Shay finished catching up with her family's news, toured the grounds to see the storm damage, and ate lunch. Stripped to briefs and a tee-shirt, she finally fell across her bed and dropped into a deep, dreamless sleep. Nothing disturbed her for the next five hours until her alarm shrieked at six. She groggily debated with herself for a few minutes over whether to ignore it and skip supper, but she eventually decided that the boys would be disappointed if she didn't join them. Still half-asleep, she rolled off the bed, stripped, pinned her braid up on top of her head, and strolled toward the bathroom for a quick shower.

Shay's bedroom was a very large, front corner room. There was an equally large guest room at the opposite front corner, and they were connected by an oversized bathroom Phyllis had extravagantly redesigned, influenced by a photo layout in *House Beautiful*, when she and Aaron had re-modeled and updated the house. Except on the rare occasions when they had a superfluity of overnight guests, Shay had this rather sybaritic bathroom to herself.

It was small wonder, then, that her mouth dropped open and her eyes all but popped when she pushed open the door and came face to face with Dag in all of his equally naked splendor. He paused with his hand on the fluted glass door of the double-sized, tiled shower cubicle, and ran appreciative eyes from the top of her head to her feet, pausing along the way to savor his favorite parts of her anatomy.

"What . . . what are you doing in my bathroom?" faltered Shay, a strong feeling of consternation rising within her that control of her life had somehow been taken out of her hands.

"Sharing it, sweetheart. When I asked Phyllis about renting a room, she said that this front corner one had the longest bed, but that I'd have to share the bath with you. Of course, I assured her that I had absolutely no objections to that arrangement, but she still insisted on adjusting the rent—"

"What do you mean you've rented a room? You can't—"

"Now, now, sweet Shay, just quiet down before you have the boys up here." Dag smiled with deliberate provocation and purred, "Would you deny me the comforts of a real home, with great cooking, a warm, motherly landlady, and a perfectly splendid bath-mate? No, no, don't be modest. You know very well just how marvelously compatible we are in the shower."

Laughing, Dag pulled her into his arms before she could get her hand on the hair dryer lying on the counter. The intent to crown him with it must have been clear in her flashing eyes.

Shay was quick to realize just what effect her struggles to get loose were having on him, and she subsided to stand in the circle of his arms, glaring at him as she hissed, "You sneaky, underhanded, devious, sly damn fox! How did you talk my mother into this? She would never rent that—"

"She did. Just as soon as I explained the situation to her, she was gung ho to do anything necessary to help me get you in front of a minister. She said—"

"What did you tell you, you Viking conniver?" Shay intoned in a voice that threatened dire retaliation.

"The truth, of course. Would I lie to your mother? Or the boys? They're going to be my family, too, and it would be bad strategy to start off our relationship by fibbing to them."

"What truth?"

"All the truth. How we feel about each other. The fact that you're perfectly happy to have an affair with me, but you're afraid to get married. I told—"

"You didn't tell them that!" she groaned, leaning her head on his shoulder.

"Certainly I did. Phyllis had already figured it out, and the boys aren't dumb. I asked them how they felt about it, and they think I'd make a great father. They explained to me that you can be very stubborn, but if I hang in, and with a bit of help from them, we'll all manage to bring you around to doing the right thing and making an honest man of me."

"Ohmigod!"

"You really should set a good example for the boys, you know. Want to say yes now?"

"No, damn you, I won't! I can't believe—"

"Calm down, sweetheart. We all know how hard it is for you to back down. We won't even discuss it any more right now, since it upsets you so. Actually, this should be a lot of fun. Phyllis and the kids have some very interesting ideas. In fact, we spent most of the afternoon in a strategy session. Sharp, very sharp, are our boys. And wonderfully imaginative. You won't believe some of the things we've planned. I can't wait to see your face when—No! I want you to be surprised."

By the end of day three, Friday, Shay realized that the whole village knew what was happening, and nearly everyone had actively joined in the "Say YES, Shay" campaign. At any other time, she knew, Dag's courtship, unorthodox as it was, would probably not have attracted much attention. New Englanders treasured their eccentrics and, aside from an amused comment now and then, let them go their own way. But now, in the aftermath of a devastating and frightening experience, everyone seemed to need a lighthearted diversion, and Dag Haldan's very public pursuit of her was striking just the right note.

The Beech Villagers got their first inkling of what was happening at nine o'clock on Friday morning when two crates of bunched parsley appeared in Ev Stoner's general store under a large, hand-lettered sign reading, "Free Samples—Help Us With Our Survey—Shay MacAllister Claims Parsley Makes You Sexy—Let Us Know What You Think—Call Phyllis MacAllister or Dag Haldan at 6300."

The newly restored phone service almost overloaded as people called back and forth trying to find out what was going on. Matters became clearer at ten-thirty when a petition was prominently displayed next to Ev's cash register with another sign: "Please sign our petition. Thank you, Marcus and Kyle Severin."

The petition read: "To Shay MacAllister Severin. We the undersigned agree with Marcus and Kyle Severin that Dag Haldan, also known as the Norseman, would make a fantastic and awesome father, and that you should forthwith say YES to his proposal of marriage." It had quite obviously been printed by one of the boys.

By noontime, Marcus, Kyle, and several of their friends were bicycling out along the country roads with copies of the petition, stopping at every house to collect signatures.

At shortly after three that afternoon, Dip and Crusher pulled into Shay's driveway in Dip's van. Dag joined them, and they loaded Shay's aluminum extension ladder on top of the van and drove back around the Green to begin their project at the station. An hour later, all available residents were strolling around the Green admiring the banners that had been strung between buildings, across the front of the station, and between trees. Dip and Crusher, at Dag's request, had enlisted a horde of college students to prepare the colorful banners that morning, and now Shay, standing in front of the station, stared in disbelief at their handiwork. She was surrounded by such messages as: "Say YES, Shay!" "Be My Valkyrie, Shay!" "Every Woman Needs a Norseman!" "Viking Liking Lasts—Go For It!"

Over the weekend, days four and five, both the campaign and community participation in it intensified. The state-of-emergency decree was lifted for the central and western portions of the state, and non-essential road and air traffic was again allowed into the area.

Dag, Marcus, and Kyle returned from a mysterious trip Saturday afternoon and promptly began distributing bumper stickers and peel-and-stick labels reading, "Say YES, Shay" or "Be His Valkyrie." Saturday evening, Phyllis, Dag, and the boys invited the neighborhood to an impromptu patio party, and Shay was beseiged with advice, both teasing and serious. She also watched with considerable interest the acceptance accorded Dag by her lifelong friends and neighbors.

"You fit in with everyone as if you'd been born here," Shay commented later as she wandered, clad only in her tiger-patterned briefs, into the bathroom where he was shaving.

"I keep telling you I'm lovable," Dag murmured, turning off the shaver and setting it on the counter. He pulled her into his arms and nuzzled her neck, distracting her attention while he deftly unbraided her hair. "You've got too many clothes on, sweetheart. Why don't you take those kinky pants off and come to bed so I can try once again to convince you of just how lovable I am? Witch! Don't pinch me there!"

On Sunday the phone calls and telegrams started coming in from MacAllister relatives in all parts of the country. When Shay, in laughing exasperation, demanded to know how they'd all found out about Dag and the bet, Phyllis muttered, "The telephone is a wonderful invention," and dashed out the door. Marcus and Kyle spent the afternoon in the third-floor playroom, but refused to discuss what they were doing and tacked a large "Keep Out" sign on the door at the foot of the stairs.

On Monday, day six, Shay received forty-three cards and letters whose main message was "Say YES, Shay," plus a long, warm letter from Dag's sister inviting all of the MacAllisters to New Hampshire as soon as it could be arranged. Dag and the boys disappeared again for much of the day, but some kind of message must have been passed around the village because every local vehicle that went through the center sounded its horn in the shave-and-a-haircut rhythm. Shortly after three, the disc jockey on the local radio station gave a brief but amusing account of Dag's pursuit of Shay, reminding listeners of Dag's fame as a pro basketball player and referring to Shay as "Beech Village's most outstanding scenic attraction." He then proceeded to dedicate one set of love songs every hour "To my reluctant Valkyrie from Dag." Shay wondered if it were possible for a man to swallow a microphone.

Late Monday night, Dag stretched out comfortably on Shay while he caught his breath and whispered in her ear, "Don't give in too soon, sweetheart. I've never enjoyed anything as much as persuading you to change your mind." Shay bit his neck.

At seven-thirty Tuesday morning, day seven, the fire whistle on top of the town hall blew a "rally" call. Within a couple of minutes, all the residents in the center were gathering on the Green, and cars were speeding in from the country roads.

Shay looked at the milling crowd, turned to Dag, and wailed, "*Now* what have you done?"

Before he could answer, cries of "Look! Look up there!"

and "Oh, aren't they beautiful!" came from the crowd, and Shay spun around to follow the pointing fingers and look up at the western sky. Four brilliantly colored hot-air balloons were drifting silently, except for the whoosh of their gas burners, toward the village. As they floated diagonally across the Green, their waving occupants began scattering handfuls of leaflets behind them in a tumbling trail. Marcus and Kyle raced around picking up one sheet of each color— blue, yellow, and green—and brought them to Shay, handing them over with sly smiles and an exchange of winks with Dag.

The blue sheet carried the message: "I can't promise you forever, but I'll guarantee fifty years!" The yellow sheet said: "Say YES, Shay!" The green sheet proclaimed: "Every Viking needs his Valkyrie!"

Crumpling the papers in her hands, Shay turned to Dag with fiery purpose gleaming in her eyes. She advanced on him growling, "You're going to eat these!" Laughing, Dag feinted to the left, spun around to his right, and raced across the Green toward home, calling back, "You've got to catch me first!" To cheers and whoops of encouragement, Shay tore after him. By the time Marcus and Kyle caught up to them, Dag had Shay pinned against the kitchen counter and was taking his time kissing her back into a good mood. "More mush," Kyle muttered disgustedly as he skipped past them on his way to the table and the rest of his breakfast.

chapter 13

THOSE WORDS KEPT revolving in her mind: "I can't promise you forever, but I'll guarantee fifty years!" Wasn't it forever that lovers kept promising? Wasn't that supposed to be the ultimate vow? But, then again, how could anyone make a promise like that when no one could truly define "forever"? Is that what Dag was trying to tell her—that he wouldn't promise anything he couldn't be sure of delivering?

If so, it meant that he was secure in his own mind about how he felt. He was not the kind of man who would promise faithfulness, steadfastness, and love for a lifetime unless he was positive that his feelings would endure. In their mid-night conversations, he'd admitted freely that he'd had a number of liaisons over the years, but was adamant in his stand that none of them had come close to being serious. "No matter how much I liked a woman and enjoyed making love with her, there always seemed to be something missing, something that kept me from being able to say, 'I love you and I want to spend my life with you,'" he'd said, and she believed him. But he'd said the words to her, and he was continuing to say them in every way he could think of.

Shay knew that she believed in his love. Last night, resting beside him in the afterglow of making love, she'd even told him that she believed him. And now, staring at the words on the leaflet, she was even more convinced of his feelings. What she wasn't quite sure of yet was whether or not she could truthfully say to him, "I love you and I know I always will." She'd believed it before with Cary, but it hadn't lasted. And this was all happening so fast. Could she trust her feelings this time?

It all kept spinning around in her mind throughout the morning and early afternoon in between the myriad distractions of a working day, plus the additional interruptions resulting from Dag's campaign. Kyle stopped by in mid-morning to tell her about the pile of letters and cards waiting at the post office when he went to pick up the mail. He'd had to get a carton from Ev Stoner to carry it all home. The Amherst newspaper provided some relief from the death and disaster news with a boxed story on the front page headed: "Dag Loves Shay and the Whole World Knows It." The disc jockeys continued their hourly dedications. Two-thirds of the cars that went past the station sounded their horns, and many drivers yelled, "Say YES, Shay." Perfect strangers stopped for gas and offered either free advice or, in the case of a few men, an alternative proposition—a foolhardy move they quickly regretted. The telephone wouldn't stop ringing.

By three o'clock Shay had had it. She turned the station over to Art McCormick, collected Dag and the boys, and went swimming at a friend's private pond.

"Remind me never to take you to a public beach when you're wearing a bikini," Dag commented as he dropped down beside her on the blanket and ran an appreciative eye over her nearly naked figure, "unless we've got half a dozen off-duty troopers with us to guard that body."

"You mean you can't take care of my body by yourself?" she teased.

Dag glanced at the boys racing each other across the pond and then up at the house clearly visible above a sloping meadow. "Mmm. Too public. Ask me again tonight, and you'll find out just how well I can take care of your body."

"More promises," sighed Shay, and then she quickly rolled out of reach, coming to her feet and running into the water with a war-whooping Dag two steps behind her.

It was after five when they got back to the house, and Dag pushed her firmly toward the stairs. "Never mind the station. We'll take care of it. You go take a nap. We've got dinner reservations at the inn for eight o'clock, and it's going to be a late evening."

Shay balked at the foot of the stairs and turned to ask suspiciously, "What are you cooking up this time?"

With an infuriatingly bland smile, he leaned to whisper in her ear, "Nothing you won't enjoy. You seem reluctant to leave my side, darling Valkyrie, or are you hinting that you'd like me to join you for that nap?"

It's not going to be all your way, you sly tease! With a spurt of method acting that would have put Brando to shame, Shay widened her eyes to limpid sea-pools of twelve-year-old innocence, slid her arms slowly around Dag's neck, and kissed him softly on the mouth.

Evidently not at all sure where this was leading, he stood very still with his hands resting lightly on her hips and waited her out. Shay, with a mental howl of glee, suddenly intensified the kiss, opening his mouth for the teasing exploration of her tongue, and simultaneously locked her arms around his neck and brought the full length of her body against his with a sinuous wriggle, pressing one taut thigh firmly against his groin.

She knew Dag was momentarily stunned. So far in their love-making she had held back from making the first move. Once she was aroused, she was as eager and even, sometimes, as aggressive as he wished her to be. But this was the first time she'd made a deliberate advance to him, and it caught him completely by surprise. Soon, however, he moved to hold her closer.

With great effort, Shay had managed not to go off into her usual state of muzzy-mindedness when kissing him. Therefore, at the first hint of his arms going around her, she was able to spin away and start leaping up the stairs three at a time, laughing exultantly and caroling, "No thanks, my helpful Viking. She who naps alone naps longest!"

Not hearing the expected thuds of his steps behind her, Shay paused at the top of the stairs and looked down. Dag stood where she'd left him, feet apart, hands on hips, gazing up at her with a smile that promised the imminent end of basic lessons and a fast graduation to the advanced course. His husky drawl of "Better make that a good nap; you're not going to get much sleep tonight," sent her running down the hall to her room humming "Tonight."

By the time Phyllis woke Shay from her nap, she had barely time enough to shower and dress—and absolutely no time at all for arguing when she caught sight of the dress Phyllis took out of the closet.

"You can't wear that bra with this. Take it off, dear," Phyllis said briskly, cutting off her daughter's sputtering protests and not giving her a chance to get out a complete word. "It's all right. The bodice is lined, and you're nice and firm anyhow. You don't really need that petticoat, either, but I suppose it won't do any harm. No, dear, there's no time to argue. Dag's waiting, and you don't want to be late. Now, there, fine, just straighten the top and...good. Stand still, dear, so I can zip this, and here's the belt. It just ties. Yes, a double knot, I think. Lovely. Oh, that's just right for you. Look!"

Carefully avoiding Shay's fulminating glare, Phyllis pushed her around to face the long mirror. Still talking a mile a minute, Phyllis hurried back to the closet to find the correct shoes while Shay stared at her reflection with an arrested expression on her flushed face.

"I've never seen you look so elegant, dear. That cream and gold against your tan is stunning, and it certainly sets off your hair and eyes. Ah, here they are. Remember those gold sandals with the spike heels that I bought on such a good sale and you said you'd never be able to wear? Well, you were wrong for once. They're just perfect for that dress, and you can certainly wear them with Dag, even with your hair all up in that swirly thing on top of your head. Isn't it nice he's so lovely and tall? Here, put these on and let's see how you look."

With a sardonic smile at her nervous mother, Shay slipped into the sandals and turned back to the mirror. She had never been particularly interested in clothes, opting for comfort, usefulness, and reasonable cost. Not that she didn't like to look good, but for years, both through necessity and for lack of ready cash, her priorities had put the self-indulgence of expensive clothes for herself at the bottom of her list. However, she was far from blind, and the reflection in the mirror of an elegant, almost beautiful, woman lit her face with a smile of pleasure.

The smile slowly turned to a frown as she looked more closely at the cream silk dress with its softly shirred bodice enhancing the firm shape of her breasts, and its skirt swirling gracefully over her hips to froth around her knees as she moved. Its only decoration was the gold silk braid that edged the low bodice and formed the narrow shoulder straps, with another, tasselled, length used as a belt.

Her eyes met her mother's slightly guilty gaze in the mirror, and she said softly but insistently, "Mother, if I'm not mistaken, this is real silk. It also looks like a designer dress and very expensive. I don't suppose you'd like to tell me where it came from, would you? It must have cost our entire clothes budget for the next six months, and I've still got to get more than half the boys' school things."

"Oh, Shay, please don't fuss," Phyllis said, nervously fluttering around the room, straightening the rumpled bed, and picking up Shay's discarded clothes. "I had such a good time today shopping for that dress, and it's so perfect for you, and—"

"Mother! It's beautiful, and I love it, but we simply can't afford a dress like this. Now, help me out of—"

"No! You can't. Oh dear, oh goodness, you just can't. It . . . it's all paid for and I lost the sales slip and—"

"Mother!" Shay held up an imperative hand and fixed her mother's wavering eyes with an equally imperative glare as an unwelcome thought occurred to her. "Did that—"

"Pushy Viking buy your dress?" Dag's voice came from the connecting door to the bathroom, and Shay swung around to find him leaning casually against the doorjamb, giving her an appreciatively assessing once-over. "As a matter of fact, I did. No, no, don't thank me, darling. It's a gift of love. Call it a proposal present if it makes you feel better, and I don't want any arguments. We haven't got time if we're going to get there before our guests arrive. Let's see, you need something with that," he murmured as he strolled over to her dresser and opened her jewel case. "Ah, just the thing," he exclaimed, handing her a pair of gold hoop earrings. "Do close your mouth, sweetheart, and put these on. The dress is perfect, Phyllis. Thank you. Turn around, Shay, while I fasten this," he said firmly as he opened a small box he'd taken from his pocket.

Dag stepped behind Shay and, before she could move away, he'd slipped a gold box chain around her neck and secured the clasp. They were facing the mirror, and Shay leaned forward to get a closer look at the gold Viking ship suspended from the necklace. Her expression of frustrated temper gradually dissolved into questioning wonder as she met his reflected eyes and read their message of love, admiration, and a very male satisfaction at having provided something beautiful for his lady.

Shay felt the last of her resentment at his highhandedness fade, and she turned into his arms with a lovingly understanding smile. "I'm sometimes slow on the uptake," she admitted ruefully, a very uncharacteristic note of apology in her voice. "Another case of lack of experience, I guess. I've never received love-gifts from a man, and I didn't understand what it was all about. Thank you, Dag, for the dress and the necklace and, most of all, the thought. They're all beautiful."

"And so are you," she added as she turned her head to glance at his reflection, admiring the way the sand-tan slacks, cream silk shirt, and tobacco-brown silk jacket set off his broad-shouldered, lean-hipped build.

For a long moment he held her close, his lips pressed to her neck. Lifting his head, he gave her a wickedly sensual smile as he said, "One thing I'll say for you, Valkyrie, is that you're the world's fastest learner."

"Only with the right teacher," she purred as he led her out the door.

With laughing evasion Dag parried all her questions about the evening ahead during the drive to Amherst, so it was with complete surprise that Shay walked into a private dining room to be greeted by a chorus of "Say YES, Shay!" from almost thirty people. Within a few minutes, Shay was surrounded by off-duty State Troopers and their wives or girl friends, all of whom were long-time friends; three of her MacAllister cousins and their mates; Dag's partner, Dan Crawford; and several towering men who turned out to be former teammates of Dag's.

Aside from family or village gatherings, Shay had attended very few parties in her adult years. A light drinker, she preferred an evening spent with a few friends to large, noisy crowds. Therefore, there was genuine amazement in her voice when she turned to Dag late in the evening and exclaimed, "I'm having a marvelous time! You're a pussycat of a Norseman for arranging all this. I can't believe your friends came all the way from the west coast for a party."

"All of them didn't. Remember, it's off-season, so they were all over the place. A couple of them were even right here in New England. They're a mad bunch, and they would have gone even farther to meet you."

"Good heavens, why?" asked Shay with a puzzled frown.

"The ultimate curiosity," intoned a deep bass voice from above her head.

Shay tipped her head back and up, meeting the amused eyes of Gabe Peterson, who was standing just behind her. One of Dag's closest friends, Gabe had been his roommate when the team was on road trips. He and Shay had taken to each other right away, and she had happily agreed to Dag's suggestion that they invite Gabe to stay at the house for a few days. She had blandly ignored Dag's rider that "It will save him making another trip for the wedding."

Laughing up at Gabe, who topped Dag by two inches, Shay asked, "And what is the ultimate curiosity?"

"To meet the woman who finally knocked the Norseman out of the game," Gabe rumbled. "And now that I have, I can see that the poor little feller never had a chance. My only complaint is that he saw you first."

"Thank you, kind sir," Shay said demurely, dipping in a mock-curtsey to one of the few men she knew of who could possibly refer to Dag as "little."

By the time the party broke up, Shay and Dag waited for Gabe to collect his things, and they got back to Beech Village, it was early morning, and even later before Shay and Dag drifted off to sleep in each other's arms. Nevertheless, Shay's internal clock woke her up as usual at six-thirty, and, despite a strong desire to stay right where she was, she resolutely untangled herself from Dag without waking him and got ready to open the station at seven.

It was Wednesday, day eight, and as she took care of the early morning customers, she wondered what Dag had planned for this day. She also spent a few minutes in amused contemplation of Marcus's and Kyle's reactions when they discovered who was sleeping in the guest room across the hall from Kyle's room. Gabe was another of their "awesome" basketball heros, and they'd been ecstatic when they found out he was one of Dag's best friends, coaxing him repeatedly for stories of the pranks they used to play while out on road trips.

When Dag pulled his big station wagon up to the pumps late that morning, Shay greeted him in a mood best described as exasperated good humor, which changed to outright laughter as she watched Gabe unfold himself from the front seat and the mad scramble through the back doors of Marcus, Kyle, and half a dozen of their friends. While Marcus filled the wagon's gas tank, the other boys clamored around Shay, urging her to agree to a proposed cookout that evening.

"It's for a gang of the kids and Dag's friends," Kyle explained, bouncing with excitement. "We're going to meet them now, and Dag's got permission for us to use a gym, and we're all going to play basketball, and they're all going to come back here after, and Nana says it's okay with her if it's okay with you, and you'll have a great time, Mom, so say it's okay." Kyle ended on a gasp as he ran out of breath, and it was two pants later before he managed to add, "Please!"

Before Shay could do more than look inquiringly at Dag and Gabe, the rest of the boys were adding their pleas. "Say YES, Shay!" "It's going to be great, Shay, and your ma said she didn't mind." "You gotta say okay, Shay. Do you know who else is gonna be here? Hamhand Flixton and Tony Stanelski." "And Roaring Roger Mallen." "And Phil Parker. Oh, Shay, you wouldn't want to miss it, would you?"

Shay threw her head back and yelled, "Hold it!" which brought immediate wide-eyed quiet.

Amused, calculating aquamarine eyes swept over the eager young faces, and the boys started to grin, recognizing the look and anticipating her next words.

"Okay," she said briskly, raising a quick hand to still the incipient cheers as she added the expected rider, "On condition that you guys help get everything ready, and you do the cleaning up afterwards. Deal?"

"Deal!" shouted the boys in a well-practiced chorus.

Amid laughter and enthusiastic thank-yous, the boys piled back into the wagon, leaving Shay with the two grinning men who were leaning against the front fender.

"Now, for your part in this," stated Shay, facing them with her hands on her hips in a challenging stance, "you're responsible for the food, and I hope you've got lots of the wherewithal on you because we're going to need," and she paused to raise a hand to tick off items on her fingers, "a couple of cows' worth of hamburger, piles of hot dogs, baskets of rolls and buns, cases of soft drinks, buckets of ketchup, mustard, and relish, a couple of cartons of potato chips, stacks of paper plates and napkins, plas—"

"Whoa!" cried Dag. "We aren't planning to feed an army. Just the boys and half a dozen basketball players, who have big appetites, granted, but—"

Shay looked at him pityingly, slowly shaking her head, as she broke in to explain the facts of village life.

"Dummy," she crooned affectionately, "you don't really think you're going to be able to sneak a bunch of famous pro athletes in here and not have everyone in the village know about it, do you? The boys will tell their families, and all the fathers and brothers will drop over, followed rapidly by their sisters and mothers who aren't about to be left out of anything. Within ten minutes, guaranteed, everyone in town will know, and we'll have carloads of people dropping by before the charcoal—by the way, don't forget to pick up a few bags—is even ready. I can tell you now just what they'll say. 'Hi, Shay, Phyllis . . . such a lovely evening. Just thought we'd stop by. Oh my, we didn't realize you had all this company. We just wanted to find out how the courtship's coming along, and—' And then it's the polite thing to urge them to stay and eat because, of course, there's plenty to go around. It's not funny, guys," Shay chided as Gabe and Dag broke up in laughter.

"Sounds like it's going to be one blast of a party," Gabe rumbled. "I can't wait."

"Don't worry, sweetheart," Dag said reassuringly, pushing away from the fender and standing close to her, his arms sliding familiarly around her waist. "Now that you've warned us, we'll take care of everything."

For a few moments as she gazed into the warm sherry

eyes, the chattering boys, Gabe, the station, and everything else faded out, and she was only aware of the soft brushing of the hair on his bare legs against hers and the smooth, heated skin stretched over the firm muscles of his arms under her kneading fingers. The spell was broken by the glint of mischief that flashed in his eyes as he lowered his head to feather a kiss on her earlobe.

She gave Gabe an impish look as Dag whispered in her ear, "If you have a tall, feisty, female cousin handy, how about inviting her? Gabe's first string all the way, and he deserves a mad MacAllister of his own."

"As a matter of fact," Shay said thoughtfully, "I do."

Suddenly she started laughing, stepped backwards, and turned around, swinging her long braid out of the way so that he and Gabe could read the news that "Redheads Love Longer" on the back of her tee-shirt.

She murmured so that only Dag could hear, "Tabitha the Terrific is five-ten, twenty-six, has chestnut red hair, and manages a karate school." She glanced at the unsuspecting Gabe, whooped with laughter, and gasped, "Atta way to go!"

Shay carefully neglected to mention that Cousin Tabitha was a retired model with a warped sense of humor, that the karate school belonged to her brother and her management thereof consumed only ten hours a week, and that from September to May she was the hostess of a weekly radio talk show broadcast from Boston and called "The New Women of the Eighties." Shay knew she was home in Northampton right now because Tab had called her this morning with news bulletins and witty remarks about Norsemen and Valkyries.

Deciding to change the subject before she gave something away, Shay proceeded to relay the latest news items to Dag and Gabe. In a singsong voice she recited, "We've got two sacks of mail cluttering up the post office, *and* the Northampton paper ran a story with pictures of us last night, *and* the Boston and New York papers had stories this morning, *and* a reporter from some sports magazine was here this morning, *and* the disc jockeys are still doing their thing for you, *and* I'm taking the phone off the hook."

Laughing, Dag kissed her on the mouth, Gabe kissed her

cheek, and the men climbed into the wagon. As Dag started the car, Gabe leaned out the window and judiciously ran his eyes from Shay's denim cutoffs down to her sneakers. Dag pulled out onto the road, and Gabe, still hanging out the window, bellowed, "Great legs, Shay!"

"Just you wait, Gabe," Shay muttered as laughter and shouts of agreement echoed from around the Green. "Oh Lord, they must have heard that halfway to Amherst. Tabitha, you weird witch, you'd just better still be home," she growled as she headed for the phone.

Shay spent a productive fifteen minutes plotting with her favorite cousin and then settled down to cope with the rest of the day. Her mother stopped by on her way to the store to tell her Dag had called, and everything was taken care of for the cookout. After twenty fruitless minutes of trying to guess what "everything" meant, she gave up and concentrated on replacing the universal joint on Bill Gray's old Ford.

Shortly after noontime an oversized pickup truck pulled up in front of the bay doorway. Shay, on her way back from answering the phone yet again, glanced at the truck, noted the "Pioneer Valley Nurseries" on the door, and assumed the driver was looking for directions. Changing the direction of her long-legged stride, she headed for the truck, calling, "Can I help you?"

The bare-chested young Adonis behind the wheel took a minute to look her over, his lips pursed in a silent whistle before grinning at her with what looked like a yard of perfect white teeth. He drawled suggestively, "If you're Shay MacAllister, you can."

Laughing, Shay clucked her tongue at him chidingly and admonished, "Behave yourself, sonny, before I flatten all your tires and lock the air pump. You've got...hmm...five seconds to give me a legitimate reason for being here. One...two..."

"Okay, okay. I've got a delivery for you," he said hastily, evidently not quite trusting the glint in her eyes.

"A delivery of what?" she asked with understandable suspicion in view of Dag's recent activities.

"Rose bushes," answered the driver, jerking a thumb over his shoulder.

"Rose bushes?" she gasped. She took a couple of steps so she could see into the back of the truck, and, sure enough, it was packed full of rose bushes. "I didn't order any rose bushes," she said faintly, looking at the driver for enlightenment.

"I'm supposed to give you this," he said, holding out a square blue envelope.

Shay took it from him and walked a few paces away, turning her back to the truck. Slitting the envelope, she pulled out a card with a charming still-life watercolor of a vase of red roses on the front. Opening it, she read, in Dag's handwriting, the message: "With luck, a bouquet of roses will last a week. With careful tending, a rose garden will last for fifty years and beyond—like our love. Dag."

The words blurred as Shay stared at them, and she automatically blinked to clear her vision, not even aware that her eyes were filled with tears. For several minutes she stood immobile, reading the words over and over as the full meaning of Dag's gift gradually sank into her stunned mind.

He didn't waste time promising me a rose garden . . . he just up and gave it to me . . . for love . . . for us . . . to last as long as we do . . . it takes love, abiding love, to think of something like that . . . careful tending . . . by both of us . . . he'll be here . . . he'll always be here . . . like love . . . oh, yes . . . yes, yes, YES!

Young Adonis was becoming impatient, and he had one hand on the horn when Shay slowly turned around to give him instructions.

For a long moment Shay gazed fondly at the banners and signs displayed on the Green and from the buildings along the outer edge of the road bordering it. Gradually, she smiled with pure, unmitigated deviltry as her sense of humor and diabolical imagination began a rapid consideration of the most . . . fitting and . . . interesting . . . and, yes, outrageous . . . way of saying YES! *You just wait, my crafty Viking. Two can play at this game!*

chapter 14

"STOP IT, YOU IDIOT," Shay scolded under her breath as she eyed her reflection in the bathroom mirror. "One look at you and he'll damn well know you're up to something."

The signs were unmistakable to anyone who knew her well—and Dag had come to know her very well indeed. It would take only a single glance at the gleeful anticipation sparkling in her eyes and the smug, secretive smile playing about the wide mouth, and Dag would be on guard. And that, Shay decided with a gurgle of laughter, would not suit her plans at all. She had to get her expression under control, and there was little time to do it in. As soon as Dag got his friends who were staying overnight settled in their rooms, he'd be coming to find her.

Shay glanced at her watch, noting that it was after one o'clock, and yawned. Her eyes went back to her reflection, and she grinned at how Valkyrie-ish she looked wearing nothing but her long braids and a blue-towel around her hips.

"Hmmm...maybe you have more pagan in you than you thought," she murmured as she started brushing out her hair.

Still brushing, she moved over to the door to Dag's room and nudged it open a few more inches with her foot so she could listen. The rumble of male voices and an occasional

muted laugh drifted in through the open door to the hall.
Leaning back against the counter, she shifted the long brushing strokes to the other side of her head and tried to catch
a word or two to find out what they were discussing.

Probably this crazy evening, she thought. How could a
simple cookout turn out to be the Beech Village Happening
of the decade? Dag, of course, and his penchant for making
an extemporaneous whoopdedo out of three people and a
firecracker. She should never have told him that half the
village would show up for that cookout!

Finished with her hair, Shay swept it over her shoulders
to hang free down her back and began straightening up the
bathroom, taking out clean towels for Dag and rummaging
in the linen closet for a dry bathmat. A soft chuckle escaped
her now and then as she remembered her belated return to
the village shortly after six-thirty.

She meant to be back earlier, but there had been so much
to do and so little time in just one short afternoon that she'd
stretched her luck to the limit. Until this afternoon, in fact,
she'd never fully realized her potential for organization. Not
that she could ever have accomplished so much without
Tabitha and the rest of her friends. Thank heavens for Tab
and her contacts. She knew everyone and where to find the
most unlikely things. It helped, too, that Hampshire County
was heavily populated with MacAllister cousins. The true
miracle of the evening was that no one had slipped and
given so much as a hint to Dag. That had been her one
worry, especially with so many Beech Villagers involved.
But everyone had managed to keep mum, and now all she
had to do was make sure Dag would sleep until morning.

*A pure pleasure . . . to exhaust him enough . . . on the other
hand, it works both ways, and I don't dare to go to
sleep . . . fortitude, Shay . . . you have a marvelous reason
for staying awake afterwards . . . but he doesn't . . . not if you
really zap him the first time around . . . mmmmm . . . now,
what . . . ah, yes . . . possible, possible.*

Shay's thoughts had most definitely taken a deliciously
erotic turn, and she instinctively rubbed her palms over her
tingling nipples as she walked into her bedroom. With a
mental admonishment to herself to get her mind back to
practicalities, she moved quietly around the big room gath-

ering up clean underwear, jeans, a sweatshirt, heavy socks, and sneakers, and piling them on the antique chest at the foot of her bed. She'd just started back to the bathroom when she heard footsteps coming down the hall. With long, silent strides she hurried through the bathroom, swinging her bedroom door almost shut. By the time Dag entered his room, Shay was busy folding the bedspread into a narrow strip at the foot of his bed.

He closed the door and leaned back against it, watching her. Pushing away from the door, he walked toward her, and she straightened and turned to meet him, her hands already lifting and reaching for his shoulders, her body taking fire from his obvious arousal. By the time his arms went around her and pulled her tightly against him, her mouth was open and waiting for a kiss.

Their hot mouths feasted on each other as their hands stroked and kneaded and gripped. Shay's towel was on the floor at their feet along with Dag's shirt. With a moan of frustration, Shay pushed her hand in between their straining bodies, reaching for the fastening of his jeans. As her fingers brushed against his belly, Dag shifted his hands from her bottom to her waist and with some effort, managed to hold her eager body a few inches away from his.

He lifted his head, breaking the contact of their mouths, and whispered breathlessly, "Wait... just a minute... sweetheart. Let me... Shay, wait..."

"You've got too many clothes on," she growled huskily, her busy fingers working the zipper down.

With a gasping laugh, Dag grabbed her hands. "Darling, please, wait a minute."

Shay looked up at him with eyes that fairly smoked. "Why? I've already been waiting twenty minutes while you put your buddies to bed. Now it's my turn," she purred, leaning forward to press her swollen breasts against his chest.

"Witch! Behave, sweetheart," he groaned, reluctantly holding her off. "You spent some of that time in the shower, and you smell delicious. I smell like a cross between smoked hickory and a brewery. That damn fool Hamhand poured half a can of beer over my head. Now be a good Valkyrie and let me take a quick shower."

He stepped away from her to strip off the rest of his clothes as he teased, "Or you could be a super Valkyrie and come scrub my back."

"Oh, no, not tonight," said Shay in a voice dripping with seductiveness while she stretched out on her side, leaning on one elbow, on the big bed. "I've got something else in mind," she said throatily as she tried to force her beautifully shaped mouth into an approximation of Tabitha's sexy pout. Her endeavors were slightly hampered by the need to hold back a strong inclination to erupt into giggles.

For a few seconds, Dag's eyes lingered on the curves of her body, and he took a step toward the bed before he looked up at her face and registered her barely suppressed laughter.

"Oh, you wretched woman!" he exclaimed as she clapped a hand over her mouth to stifle her mirth.

She missed the promise of retribution in his grin, and was unprepared when he took a fast swing at her bottom, bringing one large hand into sharp contact with her buttock before dashing for the bathroom. He was safe behind the locked door before she got further than "Ow! Oh, you—"

Rubbing her stinging posterior with one hand, Shay swung off the bed and picked up Dag's discarded clothes and her towel. *With my luck, I'd trip on these in the dark and wake him up. Ugh . . . beastly man . . . what hard hands . . . sometimes.* She scrambled back onto the bed, stretched out on her back in the middle of it, and relaxed in the soft breeze from the open windows. Listening to the rush of the shower, she let her mind drift back over the evening's events.

She had a sneaky suspicion that Dag, Gabe, their friends, and the boys really had spent most of the afternoon playing basketball, along with a couple of pickup teams of college players. From something Dan Crawford had let slip, it sounded as if Dag had dumped the cookout problem into his lap, and Dan and the inn staff had actually coped with all the details of arranging an unplanned barbeque and general wingding for a couple of hundred people on little better than five hours' notice. Dag's main contribution seemed to have been gathering up another fifty-odd participants. Oh, yes, and he shanghaied the Brushy Mountain Brass Band, unaware that Dan had already invited the Old Firehouse

Bandsmen to give a concert.

Shay chuckled as she recalled the ten-minute brouhaha between the bands before Dag settled things by decreeing alternating forty-five-minute segments. And, oh lordy, that last number when both bands joined to belt out "When the Saints Go Marching In," and half the musicians and three-fourths of the audience were flying high on beer and whatever. Since nobody in the center of the village could possibly sleep, they'd all come to the party, and there must have been over four hundred people by that time, strutting, dancing, and singing along behind the bands as they marched around the Green. What was it Dan said about those TV cameramen? Something about being in the area to film the hurricane damage as part of a documentary so he had invited them to the party.

The shower stopped and Shay looked expectantly toward the bathroom door, but she relaxed again when she heard the buzz of Dag's shaver. She sent him a mental thank you as she remembered the roughness of his face against hers a few minutes ago, and she went back to wondering about those cameramen. Not that she minded them coming to the party, but they must have shot hundreds of feet of film. Whyever would they want film of an impromptu village get-together? Unless...well, there were several well-known faces there...Dag, Gabe, half a dozen other pro players, Tabitha, and that actor, whatsisname, who was staying at the inn and starring in the last production of the season at the Pioneer Valley Playhouse.

At the sound of the door opening she turned her head and watched Dag, naked and quite magnificent, walk toward the bed. All other thoughts scattered to the far reaches of her rapidly fuzzing mind. He looked almost gilded as the soft lamplight touched the blond hair on his arms, legs, and torso. For a brief moment, just as he reached the bed and she saw his face and body hardening with his rising passion, Shay felt much as one of her ancestresses must have when she faced her Viking captor.

Nonsense! Besides, we know how those Scotswomen handled the bloody-minded Vikings, don't we?

Then, with an inarticulate murmur, he was coming down beside her on the bed, and her eager hands were sliding over his smooth skin, still cool from the shower, and lingering on the powerful muscles of his arms and shoulders coiling under her fingers as he bent his head to her breasts. Her wordless moans of delight and encouragement were half-smothered as she rubbed her cheek against his silver hair, still slightly damp and tightly curled. When his strong thigh pressed between hers, she wound her legs around his and arched her hips in a slow thrust against the steady pressure of his taut muscles. Her fingers clenched into his thick curls as his hitherto teasing lips closed over her breast, drawing the tight nipple into his mouth, his flicking tongue bringing it to a state of almost painful pleasure.

Shay could feel the deep flexures of her inner muscles and the hot moistness of intense arousal, and she twisted and squirmed to turn her body into his, tugging at his hair to bring his head up to hers. She welcomed the urgent thrusts of his tongue, closing her teeth on its rigidity in a firm but gentle hold while she played with it with her tongue. His arms locked around her back and hips, controlling her supple, rhythmic movements as her body began dancing to the age-old beat. His hand, closed tightly over her buttock, restrained the motion of her hips to a sensual brushing of her silky curls against his pulsing manhood. Her deep-throated scream of frustration was smothered by his tongue as her undulating body caught fire and she went wild in his arms, fighting his totally maddening restraint, trying to bring her legs around him and take him into her waiting warmth. As the strong, tanned, writhing bodies rolled across the bed in a tangle of long legs and swirling red hair, Shay didn't have a thought in her head—just an overwhelming feeling of determination and need to have him inside her, driving them both to explosive ecstasy.

Dag's passion had to have been blazing as high as hers, but he was struggling to prolong the inevitable mating for a few more minutes, making her savor all the nuances, forcing her to revel in his loving conquest.

A braced foot stopped their tumble across the bed, and Shay, lifting her head to draw in deep breaths, discovered that Dag was sprawled underneath her. With a half-whispered triumphant cry, she spread her hands over his ribs to pin him down. His helping hands curved around the tops

of her thighs as she lithely twisted and wriggled and settled
slowly down on him, straddling his hips and gasping with
the delight of feeling him fill her and move deep inside her.
His back arched as her hips began weaving a sinuous sensual
pattern, and his hands moved over her, teasing, encouraging, rousing her to a driving, rhythmic undulation of her
swiveling hips that he started to match when she bent over
him to flick at his nipples with her tongue. It clearly snapped
the last vestiges of his control, and with a deep groan his
head went back as he braced his feet, clamped his hands
around her bottom, and drove up into her with powerful,
accelerating thrusts that rocketed them into a mutual, star-
bursting explosion.

Shay collapsed bonelessly onto his chest, her face resting
against his neck, her breath gusting across his throat in quick
pants. She could feel his hands sliding over her thighs as he
eased her legs down to rest along the length of his, and
then for a few minutes neither of them moved.

Finally, Dag pressed his cheek against her forehead and
kissed the tender skin at her hairline.

"Ohhh, Valkyrie," he sighed. "My hot, passionate, lusty
Valkyrie . . . how I love you. You'd better hurry up and agree
to marry me before I do something drastic."

Shay was almost tempted to tell him, but then she remembered all the frantic racing around that afternoon, the
excitement of the others, and everyone's enthusiastic offering of ideas and methods. *No, not yet. He really deserves
everything that's coming to him. And besides, it's too late
to call it off now, and it would be really mean to disappoint
everyone. They're all on a Valhalla high. Patience, Shay,
just a few more hours. Oh, this is going to be a blast! A
Truly Awesome Happening!*

"And I love you, my sexy Viking. Just be a little patient.
You said I had two weeks," Shay murmured, lifting her
head to look down at him. "I've simply got to move, love.
My hair is sticking to my back, and it's hot and itchy."

"Here, let me," he said, sweeping her hair up in his
hands as she lifted herself away from his relaxed body and
settled on her side facing him.

He flipped her hair out in back of her, trailing his returning hand gently down the curving length of her side.

His fingers pressed into her hip as he pulled her closer so that he could kiss her lightly but lingeringly on her slightly swollen lips.

With a whispered "Sweetheart," he fell back against the pillows, pulling her down beside him and stretching out a long arm to turn off the light. Shay fought to keep her eyes open. At the last instant before the room was plunged into darkness, she'd seen that his eyes were already closed. She *had* to stay awake, and she desperately counted the seconds as she listened to his breathing deepen into the slow rhythm of sleep. The arm around her relaxed and slid from her shoulders, but still she waited another two minutes before carefully easing up and away from him.

Forty-five minutes later, after dressing and completing all her little tasks in the house, she was quietly closing the side door behind her. Staying as much as possible in the dark shadows of the trees, she ran silently across the lawn toward the road, crossed it, and scurried into the darkness under the trees on the Green. A minute later she joined half a dozen other silently waiting figures at the inner fringe of trees.

"Everybody here?" she whispered, scanning the group. "Great! Let's hope that wingding tired everyone out so that we won't wake them up, but let's be as quiet as we can just in case. Ready? Okay. Billy, why don't you and Peter start . . ."

chapter 15

DAG WAS JOLTED out of a sound sleep by thudding feet and whoops of joy as Kyle and Marcus raced down the hall and into the bedroom, yelling, "She said YES!" "Dag, wake up, get up, come on! She said YES!" "Dag! Mom's gonna marry you! Wake up!" "Come and look! You're gonna be our Dad!" "We did it!"

Dag had just managed to sit up when the boys leaped onto the bed and dove for him, knocking him flat again as they pummeled him exuberantly, laughing and shouting. By the time he got an arm wrapped around each boy and had pulled them all to their feet, the room was filling up with sleepy, half-dressed men asking what all the excitement was about.

"Mom said yes," gasped Marcus, trying to catch his breath. "Look!" He pointed toward the open bathroom door, and they all turned to stare at the three-foot-high YES printed dashingly across the counter-to-ceiling mirror in shaving foam.

Ignoring his naked state, Dag pushed through the throng to stand in the doorway, his eyes fixed on the three letters in stunned wonder.

"Well, man," roared Gabe, punching him on the shoulder, "don't just stand there like a rock. Find the woman! Where is she?" he asked Marcus.

"We don't know. She's not in the house, but something's going on over on the Green. When we looked for her in the yard, we could hear people laughing and shouting, but we couldn't hear what it was all about. Should we go look for her, Dag?"

"Ah, no, not yet," he said, hastily yanking on a pair of jeans and shoving his feet into elk-hide moccasins. "I want to find her myself, but you can come along."

Although early, it was a warm morning, and none of the men had thought of wasting time finding a shirt. Phyllis's mouth dropped open and her eyes widened in appreciation as her kitchen was suddenly filled with huge, half-naked males, their well-developed athlete's bodies highlighted by the morning sun pouring in the long windows.

"Look at the wall!" Kyle clamored, tugging Dag around to face a bare yellow-painted expanse between two doors. It was now decorated with another large shaving-foam YES.

"You didn't see the sign hanging in the hall," exclaimed Marcus. He ran out of the kitchen, returning a minute later carrying a two-foot-high by four-foot-long strip of cardboard with the message, "Valkyries Do It Better—Parsley Makes the Difference!"

Over the rumble of male laughter, Dag asked Phyllis, "Do you know where she is?"

"Not exactly," replied his soon-to-be mother-in-law, "but there's another sign on the side door that you should see." She grinned at him happily and waved an encouraging hand.

Everyone followed him down the short hall, stopping to read the red-printed sign: THIS WAY TO VALHALLA!

"Oh, that wicked witch!" groaned Dag. "What is she up to? Come on, you guys, I may need a cheering section."

As soon as they stepped out the door they could hear the uproar from the Green, and they all started loping across the lawn with the boys racing on ahead. By the time they cleared the trees and started across the huge open area in the middle of the Green, the hundred or so people milling about had seen them and begun cheering Dag and calling out congratulations. Pointing arms drew his attention to the new banners, and he laughed joyously as he read: "Every Viking Needs a Valkyrie and I'm Yours!" "Shay Haldan, First President of the Independent Valkyries Association"

"Dag Haldan, Preserver of Wolves" "Valkyrie Loving Is Best—Go For It!" "Another Viking Beaches His Longboat!"

"Dag, did you see these?" yelled Gabe, pointing to the small signs tacked to every tree trunk and hanging from the ends of low limbs.

"What are they?"

"It's 'yes' in every language you can think of!"

"Fantas—What in the world is that?" Dag yelped, startled at the sudden blast of music.

Everyone spun around, staring across the Green toward the Amherst road as the rousing sound of a jazz version of "Die Valkyrie" drew steadily closer. A large lavender van with roof-mounted loudspeakers came into sight, speeding down the road and straight across the ring road onto the Green. The crowd scrambled back as the van, now seen to be beautifully decorated with outer-space scenes, headed straight for Dag.

The vehicle slammed to a stop, the doors flew open, and a screaming, howling horde of Valkyries leaped out and raced toward Dag. There was a stunned moment of disbelieving silence from the spectators before they realized just what was happening and who the half-naked amazons were. Then they began cheering and imitating the triumphant war cries of Shay, Tabitha, two more unmistakable MacAllister women, and four friends of theirs.

It wasn't until the last possible minute that Dag came out of his stupefaction at the vision of eight tall, tanned, and lovely women running toward him, their lithe bodies adorned in barbaric golden costumes. They were wearing breastplates, linked around the neck and back by chains; narrow strips of glittering metallic fabric were wrapped around their hips; their flat golden sandals were held on by long gold ribbons that criss-crossed up their legs from ankle to knee; and crowning every head was a golden horned helmet. The long blond braids tossing around the shoulders of seven of the women were obviously wigs, while Shay's thick red braids were unmistakably of her own hair.

The laughing, yelping women were within one long leap of Dag when he snapped out of his bemusement, noted the coiled golden cords three of them were carrying, and lunged to one side, spinning and racing for the trees. Even though

Shay, Tabitha, and the others were exceptionally long-legged and athletic and could outrun most men, with a fraction more time Dag's even longer, more powerful legs would have taken him out of their reach. Alas, he was just two seconds too late.

Before he had taken his third stride, Shay and Tabitha—with obviously rehearsed teamwork—dove for him. Shay took him around the chest, while Tabitha executed a neat flying tackle, and the rest of the Valkyries schooled around them, grabbing for arms and legs to brake their tumbling fall. In a trice, Dag found himself flat on his back, half buried under nearly naked, laughing women.

Gasping between chuckling and trying to get his breath back, he looked up into Shay's exultantly grinning face and choked out, "You devilwoman! What are you . . . going to do?"

"Just what any proper Valkyrie does with her Viking," cried Shay, throwing back her head and yelling, "I'm taking you to Valhalla!"

The throng of laughing, clapping, cheering spectators had been augmented by early morning commuters who drove through the village on their way to work, and had, this morning, stopped to watch the show. Now, egged on by Shay's cohorts in the crowd, they picked up her last two words and began chanting "To Valhalla! To Valhalla!"

Dag, feeling several busy hands winding those cords around his legs, tried to struggle, yelling for help from his erstwhile friends. "Gabe! Hamhand! Dammit, where are you? Get them off me! Phil!" He squirmed and twisted, finally spotting his former teammates staggering around, holding on to each other and howling with laughter.

Left to his own devices, Dag fought to get at least one arm free, but eight determined women were too much for him—especially when they were gleefully bent on trussing him up like a chicken ready for roasting. He found himself being rolled back and forth as they wound the cords around his chest, binding his arms to his sides, and then taking a couple of turns around his wrists as they held them behind his back.

Nobody saw Shay wave a signal to the van driver, or

saw him speak briefly into a microphone. And between the enthusiastically chanting crowd and the blistering brasses of the jazz band, no one heard the helicopter or, for that matter, noticed its approach, until it was almost overhead. All attention was fixed on the Valkyries and their victim.

It was Marcus's cry of "Look! Look up there!" that brought all the heads up and caused the chanting to falter and die away to an awed silence. At the same time the jazz music stopped, and for a long moment the only sound was that of the engine overhead.

Almost two hundred pairs of eyes stared at the blue and white chopper and the slogan painted on its side in large red letters. Almost two hundred dazed minds slowly grasped the import of the words: VALHALLA OR BUST! Then three distinct comments broke the spell.

"Ohmigod," in awed tones. A whoop of "Shay rides again!" And finally a deep teasing voice calling, "Hey, Phyllis, I'll bet Aaron's up there watching this and laughing fit to split!"

The excited throng was again in an uproar, but good-naturedly moved back at the urgings of the McCormicks and a dozen others who had been coached by Shay in the pre-dawn hours. A large open space was quickly cleared, and, to the accompaniment of a stirring fanfare of trumpets from the loudspeakers, the chopper slowly descended and settled on the ground. The pilot cut the power, and the long rotor blades swept gradually to a stop.

Shay laughed down into Dag's face and asked, "Ready?"

His expression was an interesting mixture of apprehension, amusement, and I'm-gonna-get-you-for-this. In the last four and a half wild minutes, he'd gained new, and fascinating, insight into his beloved's creative imagination and her propensity for carrying the battle of the sexes to outrageous lengths.

"Now what, you abominable woman?" It came out as a despairing groan, but his wide mouth was twitching with the effort to hold back a grin, and his sherry eyes were gleaming with appreciative amusement.

"On to Valhalla!" Shay yelled, and the crowd picked it up and started another chant.

It was also the signal for the Valkyries to spread out along Dag's long, bound body, four on each side of him. With another well-rehearsed bit of teamwork, and before he had time to do more than yelp, they swung him up to their shoulders. Their chant of "On to Valhalla" was a shade ragged due to their tendency to break up in giggles, but they did manage to carry him smoothly to the helicopter. It was a large chopper with room for several passengers, and there was no difficulty in maneuvering Dag into a seat.

Throughout this procedure, the sports fans in the crowd, together with Dag's teammates, Marcus, Kyle, and the other boys, had started a counter-chant of "Atta way to go, Norseman!"

The seven blond Valkyries paused briefly beside the helicopter door, laughing and calling last-minute advice to Shay, who was leaning from the door. She pulled off the horned helmet and tossed it to Tabitha, saying, "You'll get the rest later." Then, with a smiling wave to the cheering, chanting crowd, she stepped back, pulling the door closed behind her.

Tabitha and the other Valkyries ran toward the spectators to get clear of the rotor blades. They pulled up, panting, next to Gabe, Hamhand, and the others, and turned to watch as the copter's engines fired and the rotors started to spin. The speed increased, and suddenly the helicopter was rising smoothly into the air, going straight up for a couple of hundred feet before angling off in a climbing flight toward the west.

"You *are* going to untie me, aren't you, love?" Dag asked plaintively as Shay secured the door and sat down beside him.

"Of course I am!" she yelled over the sound of the starting motors.

"Buckle him in first," called the pilot over his shoulder, tossing Dag a sympathetic grin before turning back to his instruments.

Shay quickly fastened their seatbelts and shouted, "Okay, Samson! Up, up and away!"

"Samson?" asked Dag, chuckling, as Shay tugged the slipknot at his wrists loose and unwound the cord from around his chest.

She handed Dag a headset and put one on herself, just as the chopper lifted into the air. Speaking into the microphone, she said, "Dag, meet Samson Embrey, always called Samson. Cousin, this is Dag Haldan, soon to join you as another poor, picked-on husband of one of those amazing MacAllister women."

Dag groaned. "A cousin! I should have known. How else could you snag a helicopter for this incredible performance? How did you manage to let her talk you into this, Samson?"

The big, sandy-haired man half turned in his seat to wink a bright blue eye at Dag. "I might have held out against Shay, but she was too quick for me. First, she recruited my wife, Sal, to be one of the Valkyries, and then she rang in Tabitha. If you think I was going to argue with *three* MacAllister women, then you don't know them very well yet."

"Oh, I do, I do," Dag assured him, returning Samson's apologetic grin with a rueful one of his own. "I don't doubt for a minute that you didn't stand a chance. Where did you get the chopper?"

"Samson owns a charter service down in Springfield," answered Shay as the pilot turned back to watch his course. "He was also very helpful in letting us practice on him."

"Practice what?" asked Dag, tossing all the cords toward the back of the cabin.

"Ahhh . . ."

"What she's trying to say," explained Samson, "is that I also let them talk me into standing in, if you'll excuse the misnomer, for you while Shay and Tabitha practiced that double-whammy tackle and they all practiced heaving me off the ground and onto their shoulders. I've got black-and-blues in places you wouldn't believe. It's a damn good thing my wife was there, or she'd never believe how I got 'em."

Dag leaned back, laughing, and turned his head to look at his chortling Valkyrie. Gazing with considerable interest at her many square inches of bare skin and her brief costume, he murmured, "Where the hell did you ever find, not one, but eight sets of breastplates? And those helmets?"

"It was Tab. As soon as I told her what I had in mind, she called a theatrical costumer and—zowie!—there we were."

"Mmmm. I'm not complaining, mind you, but between your outfit and the fact that I'm wearing nothing but jeans, just where are you planning on taking me?"

"To Valhalla!" chorused Shay and Samson.

"Okay, I'll bite. Where is Valhalla this morning?"

Shay smiled teasingly and leaned over to kiss his bare shoulder. "Don't you want to see the property you just won? Well, that's where we're going—in a sort of roundabout way."

Dag glanced down through the curving plexiglass and saw that they were following the glittering ribbon of the Connecticut River. The chopper was unquestionably beating northwards, and he knew Shay's land lay to the east. He looked at her inquiringly.

"Samson just had a new main rotor installed, and he wants to fly around for a few minutes. Then he'll take us back and drop us at Valhalla and—Oh, all right! I decided to name the place, and that seemed appropriate. By the way, what did you want it for? You've never said."

"It sounded perfect for a summer camp for handicapped children. Marcus and Kyle took me up there a few days ago, and we tramped all over it. It's going to be terrific, and eventually we could build a year-round recreational facility. You'd be great at something like that."

Shay stared at him for a long moment and then leaned toward him, pushing the microphones aside so she could kiss him, lingeringly and thoroughly.

She drew back a few inches and looked at him with glowing eyes. "You're something else, my Viking. It sounds like a fantastic idea, and I'd love it and so would the boys. What did they think?"

"They can't wait. They're already planning on being coaches for the youngest children."

Samson had been listening with great interest and now said, "If I can help, let me know."

"Thanks. I will," said Dag. "However, in the nearest

future, where you could really help is in sharing your methods of handling female MacAllisters. We should get together sometime soon. I may even have a few tips for you."

Shay opened her mouth to retaliate, but Samson got in before her, laughing and agreeing, "I believe it! You've caught the feistiest MacAllister of them all, and the stubbornest one, and you seem to have her under reasonable control—despite this morning's whoopdedo."

Again before Shay could say anything, she was stifled, this time by Dag's mouth as he pulled her into his arms and kissed her.

"Not a word," he murmured eventually. "Just answer a couple of questions. Are we going to spend the day dressed like this?"

"No. I packed a change of clothes for both of us in that bag. And Aunt Jean, Tab's mother, packed a fabulous picnic in that cooler, complete with two bottles of wine."

"Where are we having this picnic?"

"At Valhalla. There's a lovely waterfall and a natural pool where we can swim. Did the boys show it to you?"

"Yeah, I know the place you mean. It is lovely. And we won't need swimsuits, will we, my nearly naked darling?"

"Uh uh," answered Shay, laughing.

"Mmmm. Maybe I'll join you after all," Samson suggested slyly, pausing three seconds before adding, "Aunt Jean packs a mean lunch."

"I'm sure if you dropped in this noon, she'd be delighted to feed you, you poor thing," purred Shay.

She felt Dag's arm tighten around her shoulders, and she turned to look at him questioningly.

"Tell me something, sweet Valkyrie," he coaxed. "Not that I didn't enjoy rolling around on the ground with eight next-to-naked women, and being tossed around like a sack of grain, and generally being the star attraction in this crazy scenario you dreamed up, but . . . couldn't you have managed just a simple 'yes'?"

Before Shay could answer, Samson turned around to give Dag a pitying look and said didactically, "You might as well get used to it, chum. There hasn't been a MacAllister born, male or female, who can say a simple 'yes' without a paragraph of conditions. Why, I've heard my wife teaching my three-year-old daughter how to waffle, hedge, fence, dilly-dally . . . well, you name it."

"If you weren't driving this thing," Shay promised wrathfully, "I'd make your ears ring. Of all the—"

"Now, Valkyrie, be fair," Dag chided. "Even in this short a time, I've seen the evidence. On the other hand, Samson, perhaps it's a matter of asking the right questions."

"Such as?"

"Let . . . me . . . see," drawled Dag thoughtfully. He turned to Shay and asked, "You're not going to back out of marrying me next Saturday, are you?"

"No," she answered, starting to smile.

"Do you still have doubts about depending on me?"

"No!"

"You won't change your mind in six months?"

"No!"

"Six years?"

"No!" She was laughing now, and over the earphones she could hear Samson's deep chuckle.

"Sixty years?"

"NO!"

"You're not worried about my relationship with the boys?"

"No."

He gave her a speculative look. "Would you mind very much if we had a baby of our own?"

Her eyes widened in surprise for a moment, and then she grinned. "No."

"Mmmm. All things are possible, but not if you have any doubts about loving me. You don't, do you?"

"No!"

"No more fears that I don't love you just as much?"

"No."

"So you're no longer a *reluctant* Valkyrie?"

"No!"

"But you're going to insist on being an *independent* Valkyrie?"

"N—" She stopped short as Samson gave a shout of laughter. "Oh, you sneaky rat! YES!" she yelled.

"There you go, Samson," Dag cried exultantly. "A simple 'yes.'"

Shay tried to protest, but their laughter drowned her out. Then, as Samson exuberantly sent the helicopter into a sweeping upward spiral, she threw her hands up and joined in, her eyes meeting Dag's in a wordless exchange of love and promise.

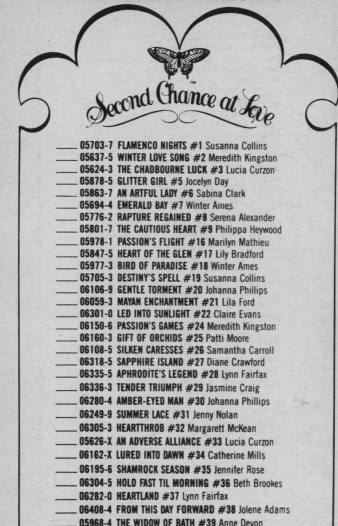

Available at your local bookstore or return this form to:

 SECOND CHANCE AT LOVE
Book Mailing Service
P.O. Box 690, Rockville Centre, NY 11571

Please send me the titles checked above. I enclose _____
Include $1.00 for postage and handling if one book is ordered; 50¢ per book for
two or more. California, Illinois, New York and Tennessee residents please add
sales tax.

NAME _____

ADDRESS _____

CITY _____ STATE/ZIP _____
(allow six weeks for delivery)   SK-41

_____ 06851-9 A MAN'S PERSUASION #89 Katherine Granger
_____ 06852-7 FORBIDDEN RAPTURE #90 Kate Nevins
_____ 06853-5 THIS WILD HEART #91 Margarett McKean
_____ 06854-3 SPLENDID SAVAGE #92 Zandra Colt
_____ 06855-1 THE EARL'S FANCY #93 Charlotte Hines
_____ 06858-6 BREATHLESS DAWN #94 Susanna Collins
_____ 06859-4 SWEET SURRENDER #95 Diana Mars
_____ 06860-8 GUARDED MOMENTS #96 Lynn Fairfax
_____ 06861-6 ECSTASY RECLAIMED #97 Brandy LaRue
_____ 06862-4 THE WIND'S EMBRACE #98 Melinda Harris
_____ 06863-2 THE FORGOTTEN BRIDE #99 Lillian Marsh
_____ 06864-0 A PROMISE TO CHERISH #100 LaVyrle Spencer
_____ 06865-9 GENTLE AWAKENING #101 Marianne Cole
_____ 06866-7 BELOVED STRANGER #102 Michelle Roland
_____ 06867-5 ENTHRALLED #103 Ann Cristy
_____ 06868-3 TRIAL BY FIRE #104 Faye Morgan
_____ 06869-1 DEFIANT MISTRESS #105 Anne Devon
_____ 06870-5 RELENTLESS DESIRE #106 Sandra Brown
_____ 06871-3 SCENES FROM THE HEART #107 Marie Charles
_____ 06872-1 SPRING FEVER #108 Simone Hadary
_____ 06873-X IN THE ARMS OF A STRANGER #109 Deborah Joyce
_____ 06874-8 TAKEN BY STORM #110 Kay Robbins
_____ 06899-3 THE ARDENT PROTECTOR #111 Amanda Kent
_____ 07200-1 A LASTING TREASURE #112 Cally Hughes $1.95
_____ 07201-X RESTLESS TIDES #113 Kelly Adams $1.95
_____ 07202-8 MOONLIGHT PERSUASION #114 Sharon Stone $1.95
_____ 07203-6 COME WINTER'S END #115 Claire Evans $1.95
_____ 07204-4 LET PASSION SOAR #116 Sherry Carr $1.95
_____ 07205-2 LONDON FROLIC #117 Josephine Janes $1.95
_____ 07206-0 IMPRISONED HEART #118 Jasmine Craig $1.95
_____ 07207-9 THE MAN FROM TENNESSEE #119 Jeanne Grant $1.95
_____ 07208-7 LAUGH WITH ME, LOVE WITH ME #120 Lee Damon $1.95
_____ 07209-5 PLAY IT BY HEART #121 Vanessa Valcour $1.95
_____ 07210-9 SWEET ABANDON #122 Diana Mars $1.95
_____ 07211-7 THE DASHING GUARDIAN #123 Lucia Curzon $1.95

All of the above titles are $1.75 per copy except where noted

WHAT READERS SAY ABOUT
SECOND CHANCE AT LOVE BOOKS

"Your books are the greatest!"
—*M. N., Carteret, New Jersey**

"I have been reading romance novels for quite some time, but the SECOND CHANCE AT LOVE books are the most enjoyable."
—*P. R., Vicksburg, Mississippi**

"I enjoy SECOND CHANCE [AT LOVE] more than any books that I have read and I do read a lot."
—*J. R., Gretna, Louisiana**

"I really think your books are exceptional...I read Harlequin and Silhouette and although I still like them, I'll buy your books over theirs. SECOND CHANCE [AT LOVE] is more interesting and holds your attention and imagination with a better story line..."
—*J. W., Flagstaff, Arizona**

"I've read many romances, but yours take the 'cake'!"
—*D. H., Bloomsburg, Pennsylvania**

"Have waited ten years for *good* romance books. Now I have them."
—*M. P., Jacksonville, Florida**

*Names and addresses available upon request